SHE WASN'T GOING TO STOP.

He'd have to do something or she'd run herself to death. Shifting himself to the left, he caught her shoulders, then dove off his horse, taking her down in the fall. The force of their impact sent them rolling over and over in the thick grass. Sprawled on the grass, he watched her scramble to her feet in a fury of fringe. He rose on his knees to defend himself as she charged him, knife ready, screaming at the top of her lungs.

There was a flash of steel, and his hand barely grasped her wrist in time and held off the small glinting blade she intended to drive into his heart.

''Hold up, you hellcat!'' he said.

JAKE LOGAN

PRAIRIE FIRES

J

JOVE BOOKS, NEW YORK

PRAIRIE FIRES

A Jove Book / published by arrangement with
the author

PRINTING HISTORY
Jove edition / December 1997

All rights reserved.
Copyright © 1997 by Jove Publications, Inc.
This book may not be reproduced in whole
or in part, by mimeograph or any other means,
without permission. For information address:
The Berkley Publishing Group, a member of Penguin Putnam Inc.,
200 Madison Avenue, New York, New York 10016.

The Putnam Berkley World Wide Web site address is
http://www.berkley.com

ISBN: 0-515-12190-8

A JOVE BOOK®
Jove Books are published by The Berkley Publishing Group,
a member of Penguin Putnam Inc.,
200 Madison Avenue, New York, New York 10016.
JOVE and the "J" design are trademarks
belonging to Jove Publications, Inc.

PRINTED IN THE UNITED STATES OF AMERICA

10 9 8 7 6 5 4 3 2 1

1

June 16th, 1877

Slocum's head hurt. Thunder roared behind his eardrums. Before he dared to half-open his eyes, he listened to the snort of a horse close by, then the sound of the animal's teeth snatching grass. Had they left? It was far better to play possum a while longer than to expose himself to a repeat attack. Those Jackson brothers played for keeps.

Through a bare slit of his right eyelid, he could see his bay horse Brownie grazing a few yards away, trailing his reins. For no apparent reason, the cow pony raised his head and peered to the east. Slocum knew a horse's vision was ten times better than a man's. There was something out there on the rolling sea of prairie that had interrupted the animal's feeding, for a snatch of long-stem bunch grass remained unmoving in the corner of his mouth. Some sort of a threat or invader continued to intrigue the animal; otherwise he would have dropped his head back down after more of the ripe grass.

1

Satisfied the Jacksons had left, Slocum sat up and began to explore his sore head for a possible crack in his skull. The knot on the back of his scalp was big enough that his hat might not fit. As he continued to examine it with his fingers, he tried to make out what the bay horse had seen out there. Some day he'd even things with the pair for this beating, he vowed.

Half-rising to his knees, he caught sight of a hatless rider in the distance. He squinted against the glinting sun to try to see more. There was a horse drawing a travois. Was it one of those Bronco Sioux? All summer long there had been reports of small bands of renegades striking outlying ranches across eastern Wyoming. The soldiers stationed at the various forts up and down the Bighorn range front had been unable to do much more than round up a few individuals. Meanwhile, it was rumored over a half-dozen of those small, fast-moving bands prowled the region. For the most part, they preyed on small wagon trains and isolated ranches.

He rose unsteadily, his head still throbbing, and stepped to the horse. From the saddlebags, he withdrew a bottle of whiskey. He took the cork out, then paused with a frown—something else felt wrong. He switched the bottle to his left hand and then reached back for his Colt. His holster was empty. He searched around on the ground, wondering if the revolver had fallen out in the scuffle. There was no sign of the handgun. He shook his head in dismay. Those Jackson twins better find themselves a deep hole. He threw his head back to swallow, and the whiskey burned as it slid down his throat.

"Damn, Brownie," he swore, leaning on the horse to steady himself. "You didn't help me one bit in that fight with those two." He looked again for the Indian rider. Nothing in sight. The individual no doubt had vanished from view over the rise.

"I guess we better get back. I wonder what in the hell that single Injun's doing out there by himself anyway." Then Slocum took another powerful drink of the whiskey, and corked the bottle with a slap of his palm.

He stuck the bottle back in the saddlebag, then walked over and swept up his weathered Boss of the Plains Stetson. The crown needed to be popped out from the blow Walter Jackson had struck from behind. Slocum reshaped the felt crown and gingerly placed it on his head. When it was set to suit him, he felt for the empty holster out of habit, then began to look around in the tangled grass for the missing Colt. Not finding it, he cursed the Jacksons under his breath.

Those brothers were plain inhospitable. They'd acted like they owned the whole country. Or at least like they owned the whole Powder River basin and resented anyone else grazing there. Maybe it had been his disparaging remark about their Damnyankee ancestry. It hadn't sounded too bad to him at the time. But then maybe they were touchy about being born to unmarried parents.

He checked the horizon again for any sign of more Indians. Nothing. Either the lone traveler was down in the next wide draw, or else he had ridden south. One Indian, all alone, pulling a travois. It didn't make much sense. But nothing had the entire day. Since leaving camp, he had been checking and counting V Bar C cattle. That was why Old Man Crawford had left him up there for the summer, to keep the steers moving to good grass and hold the rustling down. In the fall, Crawford planned to bring his crew up from Fort Worth by train to Cheyenne and then gather up the fat ones for sale. The forage across the Powder River basin stood belly-deep on a good horse; two-and three-year-old Texas-born longhorns waxed fat on the windswept prairie.

Slocum checked the cinch leather. Satisfied that it was tight enough, he swung a leg over the saddle, and then made a circle looking on the ground for his handgun. The .44 was nearly new, and he hated to ride off without it. More than likely, the twins had helped themselves to it. He still carried a Dragoon-model .31 in his boot, and an extra gun of the same caliber in his saddlebags. Back and forth he rode, searching the matted-down grass, but there was no sign of his lost .44. The Jacksons owed him twenty-four bucks for another one.

By then his curiosity was aroused enough to go see about the lone Indian. Slocum was his own boss for the summer. He reached down and felt for the smooth wooden rifle stock. His 44/40 Winchester was still in the boot under his right leg. Satisfied he had enough firepower to handle most situations, he leaned over and drew the small .31 out of his boot, then shoved it in his waistband. A good weapon, it was half the size of the .44 that he'd lost in the scuffle, but much handier in close combat than the larger-caliber weapon anyway. He'd once killed a rampaging black bear that was mauling him with the .31. He doubted that he'd have been able to pull out a larger gun and bring it into play in such close quarters.

"Let's go see what that Injun buck is up to," he said out loud, and then set spurs to Brownie.

He reached the rise, and drew up the cow pony in time to see the individual in the bottom of the draw look up at him in shock. He saw to his amazement that it was a woman. Wide-eyed, she rose to her feet and began to run, abandoning everything. Below her long buckskin skirt, her shapely calves made long strides. Thick braids flying, she glanced back in wide-eyed fear, and then hitched up her dress higher to resume her charge uphill.

Amused at her reaction, he wondered why she had chosen to run away from him. Obviously she didn't intend to be caught. He spurred Brown off the hillside and down the slope. She was three fourths of the way up the face of the opposite rise when he passed her jaded black piebald in the shafts of the travois. The horse was done in, but Indians on the move used up their mounts without much conscience. He watched her reach the hilltop, and she never looked back as she disappeared again from his view. He gave Brownie the reins. The powerful bay began to cat-hop up the steep grade.

The gelding huffed from the exertion when they topped out. Slocum rose in the stirrups and spotted the woman's flying fringe as she raced northward. He set the pony after her. The distance closed between them. She glanced back with her mouth in a tight line. Then her moccasins speeded up to try to outdistance him. Sunlight flashed on her shapely copper legs as they churned through the thick grass.

"Hold up, gal," he shouted as he drew Brownie up beside her. The deep breathing of the horse matched hers as he leaned down in the saddle to reach for her. She wasn't going to stop. He'd have to do something or she'd run herself to death. Shifting himself to the left, he caught her shoulders, then dove off his horse, taking her down in the fall. The force of their impact sent them rolling over and over in the thick grass. Sprawled on the grass, he watched her scramble to her feet in a fury of fringe. He rose on his knees to defend himself as she charged him, knife ready, screaming at the top of her lungs.

There was a flash of steel, and his hand barely grasped her wrist in time and held off the small glinting blade she intended to drive into his heart. The anger flashed in her diamond-black eyes as they struggled against each other for the advantage.

"Hold up, you hellcat!" he said, straining to hold her off him and keep the knife away. His strength drove her to her knees, and she grimaced at him, the contortions of her drawn-up face forming a mask of rage. He eventually overcame her efforts, and at last the weapon slipped from her grasp.

She gulped for air as her open mouth exposed her even white teeth. They were face to face as he held her wrists in a viselike grip. She had a slender nose for a Sioux, but it had been broken sometime before. The small rise on the bridge, he decided, gave it character. With her coal-black eyes filled with menacing hatred, she glared back at him as her firm breasts rose and fell under the deerskin blouse. A good-looking woman, but too wild to turn loose.

"You speak English?" he demanded.

She never answered, only struggled to free herself. His fists tightened on her wrists to show her she could not escape until he was through with her. But she kept trying to get away as he held her.

"Dammit, woman, I'm not here to rape or kill you! Talk to me!"

She looked away. Her dark brown pupils avoided him as if he did not exist. She understood him—he knew she did. Indian women did much of the business with white traders, and they had to speak enough English for that. Why was she so dead set against saying anything to him?

"Do you have people around here?"

No answer.

"Are you married?"

Nothing.

Did she have another knife? He didn't want a steel shaft stuck in his hide. There wasn't anything to do but put her down and physically search her. He drew a deep breath and started to push her to the ground. Her eyes widened, and she began to struggle as if her very life was threatened.

She managed to get to her feet, and her toes were beating a tattoo on his shins as she struggled. She was no small person to handle, he decided. She stood five-nine, and like most Indian women, had worked hard at heavy tasks like skinning buffalo. In the ensuing scuffle, he received several more blows to his shins. There was nothing else he could do. He caught her arm and twisted it up behind her back.

She never issued a sound, despite the fact that he knew his hold had to be hurting her. But she was out of breath, and at least his grip on her arm forced her to be still. With his free hand, he searched around her narrow waist. Next he explored her flat stomach for any hidden item, and then he ran his palm over her thighs for any bulging evidence of a weapon. Satisfied she had nothing else to use on him, he released her with a shove. She stumbled away a few feet and recovered, twisting around to face him. Picking up her knife from the ground, he tested the edge. It was sharp enough to gut a man. He stuck it inside his boot in the sheath for safekeeping.

Standing with her shoulders drawn back, she flexed her sore arm and ignored him. He took a last look at her beauty, then went and retrieved Brownie. He was still in a quandary about what he should do about her, besides simply riding off and leaving her for coyote bait. She was attractive enough to make his stomach roil like a wild river at the very thought of the ripe body underneath the leather dress. But she'd meant business with that pig sticker, and she obviously wanted no part of him.

It would be better if he forgot all about this breathtaking man killer, no matter how good she looked. She was kind of like a black widow spider. After she made love, she'd kill and then devour her lover. He wanted away from this one's web, though he'd never heard of a cannibal Sioux.

His hat reset on the back of his head, he hitched up his britches and chaps, adjusted the empty holster, then took a long hard look at the brown-skinned maiden with her arms folded over her chest. She ignored him. *Goodbye, love, I'm leaving.* He felt a lump of regret in his throat over the loss. His eyes closed, he stepped up in the stirrup and then swung the bull-hide chap leg over Brownie's rump in a deliberately slow mount.

Seated, he leaned over the horn, looked one last time at her proud stance, then took his Stetson by the brim and pulled it down. He could hardly take his eyes off her. Those long shapely hips under the yellow buckskin . . . He'd been out there too damn long. He needed to ride into town and visit some whore house for a night. Shaking his head in regret, he swung Brownie around and started west.

"Wait!" she shouted after him.

He reined up, but never turned to look at her. It was her turn to ask for help. He'd consider her request.

"Wait!" she said again, and rushed to catch up with him.

"What have you got in mind?" he asked, looking down into her face.

"I have changed my mind." Her English was good, and drew some anger from him as he considered her. If she could speak it so damn well, why hadn't she spoken to him before? Was this a plot to get on his good side and then, when his guard was down, try to kill him?

"Who are you?" He looked ahead, not anxious to get too moved by her words.

"Yellow Doe. I am a member of Sitting Bull's people."

"I thought he was in Canada." He looked around, feeling a little exposed out there at the mere mention of Custer's killer.

"My people are scattered like the wind." She made a waving motion with her hands to demonstrate that they were all over.

"Your man?"

"I have no man." She dropped her chin.

"Where in the hell are you going?" He frowned at her words. Obviously her husband was dead. Indians never liked to talk much about their departed ones.

"Some of my people are hiding in the Bighorn Mountains. I wanted to join them." She tossed her head toward the west.

"Why did you run away from me?"

She raised her shoulders, as if for strength. A large teardrop spilled from her thick lashes, then streamed down her polished cheek leaving a wet streak.

"Before—some white men—have used me," she mumbled, and then quickly turned away to cry.

Slocum drew a deep breath for strength. He tried to shake loose his saddlehorn in the grasp of his right hand, then nodded to himself over her admission. That was why she'd run away. She had every reason to dread him or any other white man, every reason in the world. He closed his eyes and loudly exhaled.

2

Wind popped the canvas sides of the walled tent. In the cool predawn, he stepped outside the flap and stretched his arms over his head. The sore muscles in his chest reminded him of the kicking he'd taken from from one of the Jacksons the day before. A fresh chill in the wind swept his face. He'd come to appreciate Wyoming. Though it could be hotter than hell one day and snow the next day, the nights required blankets, and the climate served as a refreshing change from west Texas summer heat. His liking Wyoming had allowed Slocum to be talked into watching Old Man Crawford's steers for the summer.

There was plenty of free land to graze in this country, even if the Jackson twins thought they held all the grazing rights to it. No matter. They were only two-bit players in a larger game. If another year went by with all the rampaging Sioux and Cheyenne locked up on reservations, this whole basin would be crawling with range cattle. The homesteaders would come too and try to plow it up and plant crops. He was glad the rush hadn't arrived yet. Looking around the dark camp at the chuck wagon, with the patched canvas top stretched over the bows like a ghost's ribs in the predawn light, he was grateful for the peace of the place. Beyond him stood the pole horse corral that Crawford's boys had built before leaving him there.

Where had his overnight guest gone? After they'd had a late supper of jerky together, she'd unloaded her things beyond the pen. Now, in the distance, her gaunt piebald raised his head, and the wind lifted his tangled black mane as he nickered at Slocum. *Where's your owner?* He strode around the pen, spotting her travois poles on the ground, the buffalo hide containers piled on them. Her blankets were piled on top of that. Slocum paused to yawn deeply, and stretched hard to get the kinks out of his lanky frame. No Yellow Doe.

The thin purple pink shafts of first light began to spear across the land. He turned on his heels and strode back to the campfire ring. On his haunches, he began to pile wood in the center of the cold white ashes, leftover from the previous day's fire. He still had enough wood on hand not to have to use cow chips for his cooking. But he'd soon have to replenish his stock or turn to the waist-high stack of chips brought in by the hands before they'd ridden off to Cheyenne for their train ride home.

The fire started, he let down the carcass of the antelope, shrouded in several layers of canvas and hoisted with a pulley under a triangle of tall poles to keep it above the reach of varmints. He tied off the rope and then undid the stiff wrapping. He liked beef better, but half or more of a steer would rot before he could even eat a portion of it. A small young antelope provided him with over a week's supply of meat, and once chilled out at night, the carcass stayed cool enough to last that long in his "ice box."

He whittled some small steaks out of the firm carcass, then set them aside, rewrapped the antelope, and pulled it back up. He carried the meat around to the fire. Above the wind he heard Yellow Doe's soft footfall. When he looked up to see her, she was coming around the corral in the slip of golden morning light. She only wore a blanket tied around her waist, and the first rays of the sun dazzled like diamonds on the droplets of water in her unbraided hair. Her long pear-shaped breasts were capped with ebony circles the size of Mexican dollars. They swung with her willowy walk.

"I needed a bath," she said, not looking at him for his approval as she squatted down to stoke the fire with an iron. He set the steaks down in a clean skillet beside her, then rose up. Partial nudity didn't bother Indian women the way it did a white woman. It was a natural thing to them, and with two Indian wives in his past, he began to recall how such displays affected him.

"A cool morning for taking one," he said, rubbing the sleeves of his underwear for warmth.

"The springwater in the tank is refreshing. I can do this cooking. This is work for women to do. I did not think a white man rose before the sun, or I would have been here earlier."

"That's fine," he said with an involuntary shiver at the thought of such a frigid dunking. "I've been my own cook so long, I do it out of habit." He busied himself filling the coffeepot from the water barrel. The big spring in the hillside was a quarter mile away. One never set up a camp too close to a water source. The presence of man not only frightened cattle away from the water, but also kept the wild game away as well.

The pot swung on an S hook off the iron rod over the fire as he went inside the tent for his thick cotton shirt and vest. When he returned, she was busy mixing corn meal to make dodgers, acting at home with his chuck wagon cupboard and the work board under the fly that flapped in the wind. With his galluses up, he went around and tightened all the ropes to the stakes that kept the chuck wagon shelter and his tent pulled tight.

Using a long knife from the rack, she deftly sliced up potatoes from the sack in the wagon. The snow-white nuggets on the cutting board in the half light of morning shone in sharp contrast to her bronze skin. He noticed as he watched her dice them that she lacked an index finger on her left hand. It had no doubt been taken off when her husband was killed. Many Indian women mutilated themselves in their anguished sorrow.

She showed him a handful of coffee beans for his approval. When he nodded, she poured them in the top of the hand grinder as if well experienced with such conveniences. With a grin, she began to work the handle that produced coffee grounds in the small wooden drawer underneath. Some gadget, he decided. No telling what they would think of next to invent. He wished he'd had a dollar for every handful of roasted beans he'd ground with his gun butt. In fact, cowboys would ride into camp on trail drives and say, "Give me a big slug of them gun-butt squeezings."

He scrubbed his week-long beard stubble with his palm and considered shaving it sometime. His plans for the day included riding south in a large circle. Then he paused, blinked, and looked in shock at Yellow Doe's back. In the growing light, he could see the scars on her shoulders, dark lines where someone had used a lash on her. He had some of the same marks on his own back to match hers, and the memory of the bullwhip's tail slashing into his flesh made his skin crawl.

Steaks sizzled in the skillet, her sliced potatoes browned in bacon grease, and she began to spoon-drop corn cakes into a heated Dutch oven to bake. He only wished she'd dress. The pendulum sway of her firm breasts was too distracting not to bother him. Her partial nudity made him so restless that he couldn't sit in one place. He finally went in the tent to find a cigar to smoke. When he came outside again, she looked up at him.

"I am sorry it takes so long to cook."

He shook his head to dismiss her concern, and then struck a lucifer on the seat of his pants. His hands shook as he tried to light the end of the cigar. Finally a gust of wind blew the match out before he could get it started.

The bitter taste of the wet tobacco filled his mouth. Shaking his head in hopelessness, he squatted down beside her looking for a torch from the fire to use. She lighted a long sliver of wood, cupping the flame with her palm for him. He drew in, and sweet smoke began to fill his mouth. She grinned at his success, and he nodded in gratitude. Uneasy at being so close to her, he rose to his feet. But not without another glance at her long breasts. Why didn't she go dress?

He tried to think about the old man's cattle and what he needed to do. Ride the south range, turn any of the wanderers back in this direction. If they ranged too far away they would make an easy target to steal. He watched her rise up and go for a tin plate from the table. Coming back quickly, she began to fill it with potatoes and meat, and then deftly plucked out two yellow-brown corn cakes from the oven to top the dish.

She presented it to him and he nodded thanks.

"Smells good," he said. Then, as if she had forgotten them, she went for a fork and knife for him. He settled down on a small folding chair, the plate in his lap, letting the radiant heat of the fire warm his front.

He looked for her. Seeing her standing by the tailgate of the chuck wagon, he waved her over with his fork hand.

"You get some food," he said, pointing to it in the pans. "You eat now too."

She nodded that she heard him, and then poured him coffee. He had her set the cup on the wooden crate he used as his side table, and then motioned toward the food again.

"I will eat. What else?" she asked

He drew in a deep breath. "Go put on your dress." There, he'd said it. She blinked at him as if to ask why, but with a shrug, she went at a run around the pen to her things.

Good. He studied the direction of the blazing sun. He had a long day ahead. It would be past dark before he returned. She'd be all right there. No one had disturbed a thing in six weeks. Those Jackson twins had gone home, he felt certain. At least they were miles away.

She returned in her fringed dress, and he nodded his approval when he saw her in it. Much better. After checking his plate to be sure he still had enough food, she began to fill hers. Then seated on the ground cross-legged on the other side of his crate, she busied herself eating. He remembered he still had her knife. He stopped eating, drew it out of his boot, and set the small paring knife on the makeshift table between them.

"You may need this," he said between bites. She agreed, but busy eating, made no move to pick it up. Somehow the food tasted better to him than any fare he'd managed to fix for himself in the past few weeks. There was something to be said about a woman's hand in the cooking.

He looked over as she used her fingers to gracefully slip a morsel of meat between her dark brown lips. The sun shone on the shiny traces of grease on her fingertips. A flick of her red tongue licked the spots away.

"Good food," she said, busy with her plate.

He inhaled the air. It smelled of sage mixed with the sharp sourness of the campfire smoke. In his palms, he cradled the hot enamel cup. His mind filled with many unasked questions about her past life, and he considered the wisp of steam rising from his coffee. He gently blew the vapors from the rim and then sipped on the hot rich drink, deep in his own thoughts.

"It damn sure is good," he finally agreed out loud.

3

He found the tracks about midday. From the spot where he dismounted he could see the distant purple outline of the snowcapped Bighorn Mountains in the distance. The signs in the loose dirt of the draw showed him where three riders had driven about twenty cattle westward. They very well could be some of the old man's stock, he decided as he swung his leg back over the iron-gray's rump. He had chosen Eagle to ride, turning Brownie out for the day to graze. He kept three good saddle horses at camp, plus a stiff-gaited packhorse, tying a drag rope around their necks so they didn't go too far, and rotated using them with one in the corral at all times in case of an emergency.

Eagle was fast and Slocum let him run across the flat, anxious to see if he could find more signs on the other side. The grass tops brushed his boot toes as they flew across the wide-open country. So far this season his losses had been low. He'd tallied six steers that had succumbed to diseases and natural causes and become buzzard and coyote feed. Twenty head would be way too many to lose. He needed to learn where the cattle had come from.

Standing in the stirrups, he rode down the grade at a trot. The gray was sweating on his shoulders, but not out of wind. There was no sign of anything, except a few curious antelope watching him and flicking their tails as if they were about to flee. Then a sandy section bare of grass caused him to draw up and study the tracks again. They were still headed west, and unless they had circled around, he figured he should ride on as quickly as possible and try to locate them before the cattle were rebranded and sold.

He was fixing to earn his summer wages. That was why the old man had left him up there. It might only be someone gathering their own strays, but it looked too convenient, and there had been a set of steers that had frequented the south end of what he considered Crawford's range. Especially a couple of blacks, three-or even four-year-olds, with white-tipped horns. He figured they wanted to go back to the mesquite thickets of south Texas. He'd driven them north a week before, but they had drifted south immediately and he had been looking for their familiar hides ever since.

If these riders had chosen the black, they'd learned that they weren't congenial cattle to drive in the first place, so even with three riders, the men would have their work cut out for them. Slocum never chased the quitters when he moved them. He let the worst ones drop out, and they'd simply follow the rest of the bunch back. But if a man didn't know how, he could ride his horse in the ground trying to keep the wildest ones in the herd. Of course, Slocum knew the spooky-acting stragglers would eventually trail the rest anyway.

At noontime, with the sun high above, he found fresh tracks and manure pads in the mud of a tank. One horse wore small shoes; the others were probably shod with size-twos. Homemade shoes too, he could tell from the prints. He guessed from the droppings that they were a day ahead of him.

He watered the gray in the tank and then set out in a long trot after them. It could be a wild-goose chase, but he had a niggling feeling that they were rustlers. What did the Jackson twins have to do with all this? Something was fishy. Why had they picked a fight with him? Was it to cover the theft?

It would be hard to prove they'd beaten him up the day before to let three men steal twenty head of steers. Maybe they'd figured that he might even pull a shuck after the whipping and they would have easy pickings on the whole herd the rest of the summer. He let the gray trot, and the far-away mountains drew closer.

In late afternoon, he rode beside a fresh stream. Leaning over in the saddle, he studied the tracks in the soft ground. Finally stopping, he bellied down and took a drink from the stream; he felt certain the ice-cold water came from the snow fields. Somewhere close by he knew he'd find the cattle. A hint of smoke tinged his nose, and he set the gray into a lope. On the next rise, he could see a column of black smoke that streaked the sky. Someone's place was on fire. He set spurs to the gray, and they crossed the juniper-studded flat. Viewing the tall black column coming from the ranch building ahead, he reined up to see if there was any activity, not wanting to ride in unsuspecting during an Indian raid or the like.

A house sometimes caught on fire, but not like what he was seeing. Was this the work of some renegade band? Not seeing anyone move about, he wondered if the owners were even home. He pushed the gray into a hard lope down to the bottom and eased the Winchester out of the scabbard. He held the repeater up and chambered a shell in the breech on the run. No sense taking chances. He had drawn down to less than a quarter mile when he spotted a small herd of steers. Familiar-looking critters. A jet-black one with white-tipped horns left the bunch with his head held high and ran off a hundred yards before turning back to see if he was being pursued. They were Crawford's, all right.

Slocum didn't bother with the cattle. He rode on to the raging inferno of a house. He dismounted in a sliding stop, armed with the long gun. A man's body lay face-down near the porch. Too much heat turned Slocum back from rescuing the body. Rifle in hand, he hurried around the roaring house as the roof caved in, the fiery inferno consuming it.

The body of a young girl, naked and bloody, lay sprawled grotesquely on the ground near the corrals. Shaking his head in regret, he ran past her in search of any survivors. Smoke from the burning hay in the mangers made him duck as he hurried by the pens, searching for any sign of life or of who was responsible for this butchery. In the doorway of a log shed that had not burned, the body of a boy in his teens was face-down half inside the doorway, half out in the sunlight. His back was pincushioned with arrows.

Slocum swallowed hard at the senseless slaughter as he studied the open corral gates. The raiders had obviously taken all the horse stock. He stopped and fought down the knot of nausea trying to rise behind his tongue. This had been an Indian raid.

More riders were coming. He hurried around the house, relieved when he saw that they all wore hats. They dismounted, looking with concern at the blazing fire consuming the log walls.

"What in the hell's going on here?" Walter Jackson demanded. The full-faced twin looked about to pop out of his pin-striped shirt as he stormed ahead of the others.

"Indians," Slocum said, his hands tightened on the Winchester, seeing Hansen, the thinner of the two, giving him an extra hard look. "I saw the smoke and came riding. They'd already gone." He wet his dry lips. There were several men besides the Jacksons. They looked upset at the sight of the fiery cabin.

"Is that Tom Hackberry?" one of the others asked, shielding his face, also unable because of the heat to go in after the dead man.

"There's a young girl—she's dead." Slocum shook

his head and swallowed hard to hold down the bile. "She needs a blanket over her out back."

"Not little Rachael?" one of the men cried.

"I suspect that's her, and there's an older boy with his back full of arrows in the shed doorway." Slocum went and shoved the Winchester in the boot; he'd had enough.

"That would be Tom's boy Harlin. Gawdamn them red heathens. We need to go after them."

"Yes," another cried. "Mister, you seen his wife Miley?"

Slocum shook his head. He had no taste for chasing down renegades. The small party of men could never follow those Sioux up into the mountains. The Sioux would ambush them in a minute and there would be more dead men to bury. It was a job for the military and scouts.

"You need to send for the army," he finally said loud enough that the arguing men could hear him.

' "Hell with the army. They can't keep them on reservations. We're going kill them red bastards so they can't do this again."

"Arnold, you start tracking them," Walter Jackson said to a youth with a head toss toward the Bighorns. Then the burly man squared off and looked hard at Slocum. "We ain't a bunch of yellow bellies like the gawdamn Texas trash that comes up here hogging our grass and water."

"You keep talking like that you better have a burial plot picked out for yourself, Jackson," Slocum said, realizing at the last minute that his holster was still empty.

"You talk big holding a rifle on a man." Walter nodded to the Winchester. "Next time, we'll see who the yellow one is." Walter's small red eyes closed to slits. Then he began to laugh, mocking and loud.

"Quit that, Walter." A man dressed in a business suit rode in between them. "We've got enough trouble with Injuns here. You and this Texan can settle your difference later."

"Keep out of this, Henry Clay," Walter warned.

"I said quit your troublemaking. He looks to me like he could handle himself."

"Yeah, all them yellow-belly rebs act that way until the time comes."

"Some of you come quick! I found her up the road!" the tracker shouted as he rode back. "Mrs. Hackberry is barely alive. We'll need a buggy for her. Got to get her to Doc's as quick as we can. Oh, they've cut her up and scalped her too, but she's alive."

"Hansen and I will hook some of our horses to a buckboard," Walter said, sobering at the boy's words. He gave Slocum a final hard look before he rushed away.

"Mister, what's your business up here anyway?" Henry Clay asked, riding his horse closer.

"Slocum's my name. I'm the rep for the V Bar C ranch."

"I've seen some of that brand," the man said as if in deep thought.

"There's two dozen head of my company's cattle not a quarter mile from here. They didn't drift here either. They were drove here. I tracked them and three horses."

"Are you saying Tom Hackberry stole them?" The man's dark eyebrows furrowed in concern.

"You the law?"

"Deputy sheriff."

"Mr. Clay, I don't know who moved those steers, but those two Jacksons slipped behind me yesterday and did a fair job of beating the hell out of me. Three riders brought those cattle to this creek bottom. I tracked them here."

"That's why there's bad blood between you here to-day?" Clay asked, and looked mildly after the men driving the buckboard at breakneck speed out of the yard with the rest of the men on horseback behind it.

"Yes, but I came here because of the smoke. I figured whoever lived here needed help. I found the steers a quarter mile back.'' He tossed his head and watched for the man's reaction.

Clay pinched his upper lip and then nodded as if he had considered the entire story. ''You're barking up the wrong tree if you think Tom Hackberry did that. I mean, moved those cattle of yours onto this range.''

''Maybe someone wanted me to think he did that,'' Slocum offered.

''What do you mean by that?''

''Could have been a setup. I accuse Hackberry of stealing cattle and then we draw up sides.''

''Who in the hell would win in that case?'' The deputy frowned in disbelief.

''This is your land, mister, not mine. You tell me. I've got about five hundred steers to watch for Old Man Crawford until fall.''

''Slocum—don't do anything rash. Keep this incident under your hat until I can find out some more.''

They both turned to watch the hatless Walter bring the buckboard past them in a cloud of dust, the woman and two men tending to her in the back. Slocum figured she would be lucky not to be killed in a wagon wreck as a result of Walter's wild driving.

The young man who'd found her reined up in front of Clay. ''You want me to go wire the army now, Mr. Clay?'' The other riders, looking pale-faced, stopped their horses in a circle to wait for the next word from the deputy.

''Yes, I think you better do that and then send a wire to the sheriff as well. Let him know I'll send him a report on this raid. Some of the rest of us will wrap up the bodies and take them into Mansford for burial. How bad was the woman?''

''Bad. They cut her all over and she was all bloody.'' The youth had a pained expression. The grim nods of the others told Slocum enough. She'd be lucky to live.

''Mrs. Hackberry comes from tough stock. Maybe she'll make it. Get on your way,'' Clay said to the youth.

The youth reined his hard-breathing mount around

and then headed him north. Flat out with his tail flagging, the white horse flew away across the flats until they could no longer see him.

Clay turned to Slocum. "You're going back to your place, I guess?"

"Yes, I'll pick up my steers and head back. You can find me around there if you need me."

"If I hear anything, I'll send you word."

"I'd appreciate that," Slocum said, and stepped up in the saddle. "I guess those Jacksons are pillars of the community?"

"No." The man shook his head slowly as if considering the matter. "They're hotheads, but I wouldn't consider them cattle rustlers."

"Just wondered," Slocum said, and gave all the men a salute. Then he rode out after his steers. Hard to tell whose side Henry Clay was on. He had loyalties to his neighbors, but he acted halfway fair under the circumstances. Only time would tell. Better get to gathering that bunch. It would be past dark when he got back to Yellow Doe and camp. Way past midnight probably.

4

The quarter moon shone bright in the east. Since it was late rising, Slocum was grateful for the moonlight when it did come over the horizon. He trotted the tired Eagle all the way back after leaving the steers near the Powder River. He must have covered close to fifty miles or more that day. Short of the dark camp, he spotted the open corral gate. He reined up Eagle and strained to see as he drew the .31 from his waistband. Sober as a judge over his discovery, he dismounted. Letting the snorting horse blow noisily, he slipped away from the animal's pearl outline in the moonlight.

Where was she? Had she taken Brownie and left? Some trade she'd made with him, leaving that worn-out piebald in exchange. He carefully lifted the flap of the tent with the muzzle of the small Colt. No one inside. Next he moved around the corral, listening to his gray in the distance blowing and grunting, along with a coyote howling at the moon. He found her things still piled on the travois. Strange that she would leave them and her expensive blankets behind. She'd thought enough of them to drag them from God knows where to there. Still, Brownie was gone, perhaps his other saddle horses as well, and so was she.

He went back by the corral gate and on his knees lighted a lucifer to examine the tracks. There in the dust was the answer he sought. Unshod horse prints were all about. Some buck had come that day and claimed her. One thing didn't add up for him. He squeezed his chin between his fingers. If she'd left willingly she'd have taken her good blankets along. A Sioux woman counted such personal items as her own estate. She would never have left them behind. He knew that much about Indian women. Their wealth was shown by ownership of such expensive possessions.

Since it was too dark to find out much anyway, he stuck the .31 in his waistband, then went and unsaddled the gray, leaving the saddle and pads piled on top of each other out on the prairie. Both he and the horse needed some rest. In the morning he would decide about going after her. Hell, there was no justice. Two days before he had been bored stiff moving Crawford's steers toward the river and heading the strays back into the range. Since then he'd had a run-in with the Jackson brothers, seen the bloody handiwork of the Sioux raid, and found and then lost a perfectly lovely Indian woman. He closed his tired burning eyes and began to recall her firm breasts rocking back and forth. Come first light, he would do something about finding her again.

5

He searched the distant Wolf Mountains' dark hulking forms. Obviously the Indians that took Yellow Doe had headed for them. Slocum had no problem following their tracks. They acted as if they didn't care who pursued them. They'd not done a thing to hide their tracks from anyone.

A trap? He wondered as he remounted the gray and started down the long steep slope. There was no sign of the Indians, but he had lots of country to cross to even reach the foothills of the Wolf range. The Indians could be anywhere. If she'd taken her blankets he would have said good-bye to her ghost, but the fact that she had left them behind had niggled him. He felt that the bucks had forced her to go with them when they'd stolen his horses. They'd taken the whole lot, except for her pie-bald, who couldn't keep up. So he was actually chasing horse thieves and on Crawford's business. Taking his saddle stock would have made the old man so mad he'd have chewed nails in two had he been there.

Torn between watching the steers and recovering the

cow ponies, a man had to put a priority on one or the other. His choice had been for recovering the riding stock. But now dark blue clouds were pouring out of Montana. They made the mountains ahead look almost black, and soon cooled down the sun's heat as he rode northward.

All he needed was some freak snowstorm to cover up their trail, and he'd have to go back to camp empty-handed. He leaned back in the saddle as Eagle skated on all four shoes down the steep face of the mountain. Grateful when the pony's feet were under him again, Slocum drew in a deep breath. This horse-thief-chasing business would not be easy.

It began in mid-morning, a stinging rain. Under his canvas coat, he hunched up and let the gray pick his way. In less than a half hour in his world of growing darkness, the precipitation turned to ice and snow. The temperature dropped thirty degrees, and he wasn't even halfway certain this search would be a success. Head down, the ice pellets thudding on his tall hat, he rocked back and forth in the saddle hoping Eagle knew more than he did about where they were headed.

He watered Eagle in a small stream and then, seeing tracks in the mud rimmed with the white flakes falling from the sky, he headed north. It would be pure hell if he froze to death in the summer up there. He shivered under the coat and wished for more clothing.

Not seeing much more than the white curtain before him, he let the gray walk uphill, leaning over to watch where the snow quickly melted into the red ground. From the sign, he knew the horse thieves had come this way. But how long ago, or how far ahead of him they were, he wasn't certain. He turned his face away from the sharp wind and let the pony pick his way. The gelding acted as if he knew something as he pushed into the wind. Eagle might be scenting his old pals. Slocum hoped so, because with the storm cutting his visibility down to a few yards, he doubted he would be able to find much, and might even ride by the thieves.

They crossed a low front range, the snow still coming more in ice pellets than flakes. Then Eagle nickered and his ears went forward. Slocum quickly slipped off and caught the horse's muzzle to silence him. He listened above the wind's wail for a reply.

"Hold tight, old pony," he said, not hearing anything but knowing that he was close to something familiar to the gray. Where were they? He looked around his small snowy world. He couldn't risk riding right in—be a good way to get himself killed, and might even get her hurt.

He ground-tied the gray, not hearing another horse answer. Then he drew out the Winchester. The low sage was all that was around him, and past twenty steps was a wall of the snowfall. He eased off toward what his senses considered north, the direction Eagle had nickered in.

The rifle in his cold hands, he wished he'd taken his gloves from his saddlebags. Like a man walking on thin ice, he moved like a slow tortoise through the shin-high sage. There would not be any cover if he drew any fire. Where were they? Sometimes Indians denned up during storms. Had these? His stomach filled with a rock in the pit of it as he considered the trap he might be walking into. Then he heard a horse snort somewhere close by, and his heart rose in under his throat. His fingers tightened on the stock of the long gun. Bent low, he moved forward, and soon discovered all of his horses and some mustangs hitched to a rope line between two cedars.

Where were the rustlers? He caught a wisp of smoke. The notion of some heat formed gooseflesh on his arms under his sleeves. It was getting colder, and he shivered under his unlined coat. Then he spotted a canvas-covered lodge. How many were in there? He could see so little—but his enemies would be affected the same way.

He glanced over his shoulder. The horses were almost out of his sight.

''You are mine!'' someone shouted in a loud, heavily accented voice.

The cry of protest that followed was from a woman, and they hastened Slocum's steps. He considered his options as he hurried to the entrance flap. All he could do was bull his way in.

''No!'' she cried out as he drove in the entrance with the rifle barrel in front.

The two bucks holding her arms were hardly more than boys, but the big bearded man wearing only a leather shirt and a ready erection in his fist looked madder than a cornered grizzly at Slocum's intrusion. In an instant Slocum saw the flash of her bare leg. Then her foot slammed into her attacker's face. The well-placed kick spun the man around under the low roof so that Slocum could drive the rifle butt into his gut, bending him over, and then deliver the next blow to the back of his head.

The man went into a pile at Slocum's feet. The two young Indians crowded to the lodge wall as Yellow Doe pulled down her dress and then struggled to get up with murder in her eyes.

''Who is he?'' Slocum asked, pressing the side of the gun barrel to her upper arm to keep her from attacking the bucks.

''Pierre Deveau. He's a breed.''

''Who are those two jaybirds?''

''That one is Horse Eats Grass and he is Water Runs.'' He could see she still seethed with rage at the pair.

''They ain't nothing but boys,'' he said to calm her anger.

''I am going to make them geldings,'' she said, and he had to reach out and grasp her shoulder. The two bucks huddled together, and almost shook at her fury.

''I tell you what. First you tie them up, and then we'll decide about their private parts later.''

She turned and frowned at his demand. He returned her stern look with one of his own. And then, with a head toss, he motioned for her to do his bidding.

Deveau began to stir. Satisfied she was going to obey his orders, Slocum knelt down and disarmed the breed.

"Who are you?" Deveau growled from his face-down position as Slocum poked him with the rifle muzzle to keep him down. Meanwhile, Yellow Doe was tying the young bucks up with leather strands.

"The man you stole them horses from," Slocum replied.

"I can pay you," the breed said. "And for the woman too."

"You should have thought about that before you took them." She tossed him some leather strings to tie up his prisoner. Obviously she now had the pair bound up, for she managed to kick both of them in the side despite the low roof. Like whipped pups they huddled close to the lodge wall.

Satisfied Deveau was well tied, Slocum jerked his bare-ass prisoner up to a sitting position.

"It's cold without my pants," Deveau grumbled.

"You can freeze it off for all she cares."

"Why did it take you so long?" she asked, brushing the trash and dirt from her hair.

"It's snowing out there," he said.

"Are you hungry?" She smiled at him as if her question was in jest.

"You got food?"

"That's what I kept busy at," she said. "I knew after they ate what he would want to do to me." She nodded her head at Deveau, and then her eyes narrowed to slits as she glared at him. In a fit of anger, she swept up some dirt and threw the grit in his face.

"This is the man that hurt you before?" Slocum asked.

"One of them." She nodded, but looked away.

"I bought her fair and square. Ask those boys. I am the one who owns her!" Deveau strained at his bonds behind his back.

"They'd lie to save their own butts. How did you buy her?"

"I bought her from an army scout."

"Which one?" He knew plenty of them, and they were mostly men like Deveau—part Indian, part white, and mostly outlaws outside of their service for the military.

"Whipper Murdock sold her to me."

"Damn, girl, you have been in the clutches of the devil. How did he come up owning you?" Slocum asked, recalling the bathless Scotsman with his red beard and the manners of a Missouri jack.

"My man was killed in the fighting," she began, raising her shoulders with pride. "I was very sad for many days. I cut away this finger and did not eat. I wished to die too.

"A man called Lost Away found me and said that my chief Sitting Bull had gone to Canada to see the Queen. He would get a new homeland for the people there. There were still buffalo there. I was young and strong and they would need such women in this new land. That we must go, for the yellow legs were looking all over for my people and killing everyone for the battle at Sweet Grass that you call Little Big Horn."

"And you started to Canada?"

"We started. But the soldiers were many and we hid most of the time from the patrols. There was no food and we were soon on foot. Canada is far without horses.

"Maybe two moons later," she went on, as if recalling the details better, "we had made a lodge from an old wagon cover because we were too weak to run if the army came. Lost Away had made a bow and we made arrows. Then we ate the raven, rabbits, prairie dogs, and some prairie hens, and our strength came back. I found wild turnips and onions.

"The soldiers could not find our camp, but one night as we slept, this red-beard one they call Murdock came, crept in our lodge, and shot Lost Away in the head. The gun's blast was so loud I woke up screaming and coughing on the smoke. Then I saw the hair on Lost Away's scalp was on fire. Murdock struck me on the head with his gun barrel and you know what he did to me?'' She looked at him in the dim light of the lodge.

Slocum nodded.

"See, I told you I bought her from Murdock," Deveau said.

"You ain't going to need her where you're going," Slocum said.

"Where's that?'' he asked, affronted.

She rose and went outside without another word. Slocum took a seat on the ground. The rifle across his lap, he considered what he should do with the three prisoners.

"In Texas," he began, "we hang horse thieves and don't ask no one. In Wyoming, I guess I'll have to pack you to the law and let them throw you in jail."

His words silenced the man; the two boys looked like they were trying to let their shirt collars swallow them. The pecking of the ice pellets on the canvas grew loud. Slocum looked up as she came inside bent over with a covered plate of food for him. He set the rifle aside, knowing his growling stomach would sure appreciate the food.

Three prisoners and a good-looking Indian woman to worry about. He hoped to be back on his home range in a few days. *I even got your horses back, old man.*

6

The log jailhouse in Buffalo looked solid enough to hold them. Slocum gave the Johnson County sheriff all the information on the horse theft. But he never mentioned Yellow Doe; she had elected to remain outside town in a camp he had made.

"That was sure a freak snow we had the other day," the tall man with a beard said as he walked outside the low-roofed courthouse with Slocum. Sheriff Nigh seemed like a man who handled things.

"Sure was. I almost rode by them in it," Slocum admitted, busy untying the saddled horses he'd brought the prisoners in on. He loped the reins on the first one's horn, preparing to lead them away.

"My deputy Henry Clay was in a few days ago, and told me that you had tracked some steers up into his country." Nigh stood with his arms folded on his chest.

Slocum nodded that he had heard the man. "Did Clay learn anything about the cattle rustlers?"

"No."

"Is that woman alive?"

"Yes, but she'll be badly scarred. Did you know those devils had scalped her?"

"I heard they had. Someone on shod horses drove those steers up there. No Indians drove them steers up there. I tracked shod horses all the way."

"I believe you, Slocum. Any man can track down a breed horse thief knows his business. You seen any of them damn renegade Indians out your way?"

"No."

"You better sleep light out there. The damn army ran up in the Bighorns after that raid, and came right out without finding a sign of them."

"Thanks for the warning. You need me for their trial or anything?" He gave a head toss toward the jail.

"We ain't wasting no court time on them three." The sheriff shook his head to dismiss any concern. "In a few days in *my* jail, why, they'll be pleading guilty in no time and save Johnson County all those expenses. You caught them red-handed, didn't you?"

"I sure did."

"That's the way I've got it down. By the way, the sheriff's office usually gets the sale proceeds of their horses," he said, eyeing the three saddled ponies.

"Oh, you can have them," Slocum said, leaning over and handing the man the reins to them. He hadn't even thought about the matter. They were mustangs anyway and not worth much.

"Kinda helps us pay the expenses of feeding them while they're here in the county jail."

"Never thought of it." Slocum gave the man a salute.

"Thanks. You watch out for them renegades out there. You hear me, Slocum?"

"I will," he said over his shoulder, and headed Brownie out of town. He wondered how much work Clay had done on the rustler business. Probably not much. Slocum would have to keep his eyes open.

He spotted Yellow Doe busy in camp when he stepped out of the saddle and loosened the latigoes. She quickly came over and elbowed him aside to take over the job with a wide smile. Her thick braids were wrapped in ermine fur with small yellow and blue feathers, and hung down her back twisting and swirling as she undid the girths. Silver earrings glistened in the sunlight as she hoisted his kack from Brownie's back. He followed her toward the campfire circle and the coffeepot, admiring the swing of her hips and rear as she carried the rig in both arms.

While she stashed his gear, he knelt down and poured himself some coffee in a tin cup. There was a lot he needed to do back at the cow camp. Some of those long-horns by this time had no doubt wandered out of the country, so he would need to make some wide circuits when they both got back there. He blew on the steam from the coffee and studied the snowcapped Bighorns that lay beyond the small community. The renegades were still up there. The army must be getting soft, or else the scouts couldn't read sign, for that to happen.

"You have no woman?" she asked, kneeling across from him as if occupied with the small fire. She placed a split piece of dry wood on the flames.

"No woman," he said, his mind still on the notion of renegades, straying steers, and all the work ahead.

"Am I so ugly?"

"Ugly?" He blinked at her. Hell, she was the best-looking woman he'd seen in months, including all the white women he'd seen in Buffalo that morning. On the two-day ride back from Montana, he could hardly think of anything but her—but then he'd had three prisoners to watch.

"You think I am ugly?" Her thin brows furrowed questioning him.

"No! Why, you're pretty as the prairie flowers in springtime."

"Good," she announced, and stood up. "I wish to stay with you."

"What about your people in the mountains?" he asked, blinking at her words and his good fortune.

"They can live in the mountains."

"That's final enough. What now?"

"You should go take a bath in the river and shave your face."

"Hell." He scrubbed his two weeks of whiskers with his palm and considered her demands. "You ain't no more than moved in, woman, and you're already mending my ways. But it ain't a bad idea." He nodded in agreement and headed for his things to find the cotton feed-sack towels.

The sun was up and the temperature warm enough that he wasn't liable to catch pneumonia taking a bath. He'd not seen a soul since leaving town, and the willows along the stream made a good curtain.

"You got any hot water?" he asked, thinking about cutting off his whiskers first and letting the sun get hotter before taking a plunge. That stream was pure snow melt, and his sack almost shriveled up in his belly at the thought of the cold water.

She pointed to the steaming kettle on the S hook over the fire. He gave her a nod, then smiled before he went to dig out his looking glass and gear. With hot water in a pan, and armed with a horsehair brush and a soap mug from his gear, he went to lathering his face, drawing a grin from her.

His face hot with soap, he gave the single-edged razor a strop or two on his boot top, and then set in to cutting away the soaked growth. She held the small mirror up for him, and her brown eyes twinkled with amusement as he sliced away at the wiry growth, then rinsed the whiskers off the long blade. The small black-white islands of soap and whiskers floated in the pan as the razor's edge sheared more off at the skin.

"You may not know me without all this hair," he teased.

"I will," she said, acting satisfied that she would.

"You're a lot of trouble," he said, shaking the razor at her before he leaned toward the glass and took some more off.

She giggled and looked away at his words. Damned if he didn't think he'd embarrassed her. It was hard to tell with such a dark complexion. He studied her smooth brown cheek and the long curled black lashes that hid her eyes from him. With a deep breath, he went back to his shaving, and tried to think about something besides the ripe willowy woman only inches away. He felt swelled up inside his chest from her closeness, and wished all this shaving and bathing business was completed. With a deep breath he went back to shaving. He looked beyond the reflection and met her gaze. His hand poised for a long second as he saw the deep sincerity in her brown pupils. Damn, he better go to paying attention to his shaving or he was liable to cut his own throat.

He let the slight tremble in his fingers pass, then made quick work of the rest of the shaving. The blade was wiped off and dried, the brush rinsed out, and she tossed the water out in the sagebrush as he stowed his gear. He packed it all away, and then took the bar of soap and towel and headed for his icy fate.

A man will do a lot of not-so-smart things to win favor with a woman. He sat on the bank and wrestled with his right boot until she joined him and took over the task. The left one came off in a release that sent her staggering backwards, and they both laughed as he rose and undid his galluses.

No one was in sight, and he unbuttoned his shirt and hung it on a willow. Then he shed his pants, and that left his one-piece underwear. He looked around and paused to see that her braids were undone. Then he watched her raise the fringed blouse over her head. Her long-pointed breasts shone like polished copper in the sunlight. She undid the lacing that held up her skirt, and slipped it from her long shapely hips.

"My God," he gasped under his breath at the sight of her figure.

A knot formed in his throat as he fumbled with the buttons on his underwear and tried to watch her. Undressed, she never looked back, simply strode down the sandy bar and into the swirling water that soon was to her waist. She glanced back to watch his progress as he jerked off his socks. Then, on pained soles, he hurried to join her in the stream.

The water was a damn sight colder than he had even imagined. It took his breath as he waded knee-deep to join her, soap grasped in his fist. He was determined to not show that the chill was bothering him. The rocks underfoot were slick, and as he caught his balance, he couldn't understand how she could tread them without slipping.

Then she turned away, put her arms over her head, and dove into the deeper pool. Like a sleek river otter, she glided down the stream, and at the far edge of the eddy, she jackknifed her glossy body and swam back to him.

Holding her long hair back with both hands, she tossed the wet tresses over her back as she emerged before him. She held out her hand, took the soap from him, and began to lather his body as he stood uncertain of his footing on the mossy bottom. He enjoyed the feel of her hands working over his chest with the slickness of the suds as the high sun warmed him.

Her fingers slid between his thighs, and he caught his breath. Standing close to him, she lathered his growing root and the aching seeds behind it. He swallowed hard enough to hurt, and then threw his arms around her, drawing her to him.

His mouth found hers, and for a long moment her lips were still and unmoved. Damn, he recalled that most Indians never did kiss their women. Then her mouth parted as her warm breasts pressed to his bare skin, and he could felt the hard nipples as if they were knives. Her deathlike grasp on his root caused it to respond.

He reached to lift her and carry her from the stream, unable any longer to control his wildest desire to have her body. But his efforts to carry her caused his feet to slip, and instead of lifting her up, he found himself floundering neck-deep in the cold water with her on top of him.

Her laughter rang like a bell as he found her mouth and silenced it with his nose half-filled with the rushing stream. The firmness of her lips on his and her arms holding him down signaled the desire they both sought.

Then she rose and helped him up and hand in hand, they dashed for the shore. She towed him up the sandy bank, and he swept up a towel from the willows on the run. Scolded by several redheaded blackbirds, she showed no mercy to his pained soles as she hurried him toward the camp. Sharp sticks, thorns, and assorted other objects speared the bottoms of his feet in their haste. At this rate he would be a cripple for the rest of the summer.

Good thing that none of his Texas pals saw the two of them running stark naked like this in the daylight. He'd never live it down. She ducked in the small canvas tent, and spilled herself out on the blankets spread on the ground. He winced in pain at the last stick he'd stepped on, and then lowered his head to join her.

In a quick sweep she brushed off her soles, and then grinned at him as he took a place beside her. He tried to do the same thing, but realized it would not work in his case since he had horns stuck in his soles.

She pushed him back on a soft bed of boughs underneath the covers that he realized she had fixed for them while he'd ridden into Buffalo with his prisoners. Then she sprawled on top of him, her breasts on top of his chest. She kissed him as if seeking the same magic that had made them both so wild with desire in the stream. Her palm ran over the lower part of his stomach, and soon found his rod.

He almost went out the tent roof at her first touch. He clasped the cheeks of her firm butt in his hands and kneaded them. They both soon were lost in the tempest storm of passion, and with trembling hands he rolled her on her back. His need to have her body blinded him to everything as he spread her limbs apart and moved between them, the weight of his swollen shaft waving under him, aching to join her as one.

The smooth skin on the insides of her powerful legs rubbed on each side of his body as he drew himself closer. The sensation sent bolts of lightning to his brain. Her gates parted open as he eased himself into her. His hips ached to plunge to the very bottom, but her constricted opening resisted his drive, and he fought the restriction to go deeper and deeper each time. She raised her hips up to meet his actions, her legs locked around his waist.

From his half-open eyes, he watched the dreamy slits of her eyes as she grew more carried away with their involvement. Harder and harder he plunged to match her spirited lust. Then she threw her head back and began to cry out loud. The moans of pleasure from her parted mouth grew so sharp he wondered if he was hurting her. Then her muscular arms drew him down on top of her as he sought more and more of her. He felt the waves of her tightened pleasure close around his root in his wild ride as he gave her all that he could.

Like cougar claws, her fingernails raked his back as she arched her body for even more of him. He felt the bottom inside her, and she cried out. Her fierce internal contractions drew up his seed from the very depth of his scrotum, until the force of his effort blew apart his rock-hard throbbing knob inside her in a fiery explosion. Then, with the debilitating effect of his last plunge, with the last drop of his fluid expended into her, with his pubic bone pressed hard against hers, he pitched into the dark pit of exhaustion.

7

The next morning they broke camp to head back. Slocum felt certain his stiff back, hips, and legs would never be the same, but as he watched her scurry about in a wild flurry of fringe and braids, piling things on the travois, he figured this might prove to be a very short summer. Way too short.

In his time, he'd known some real pretty Indian women. He'd even traded for a couple of them, married some, and made love to several others, but Yellow Doe was wildest one on a blanket that he could ever recall. And she was ready to do it again with the snap of his fingers. He shook his head at the whirling memories of their fiery encounters. Feeling completely depleted, he waited aboard the gray horse, ready to ride home—or at least to his cow camp.

Brownie was the best broke of the cow ponies, so they used him to drag the poles. Yellow Doe loaded much of the outlaws' bedding and the goods she had brought via travois from Montana. Then they were ready to go. He herded the other cow ponies and two mustangs that Deveau had donated to him free of charge. He could have used the money from the other horses and tack, but he would get by. Besides, there wasn't much to spend money on out there all summer herding the old man's steers—though the prospect of having the woman in camp sure brightened his outlook on the rest of his time in Wyoming.

"What will you do now?" she asked, riding beside him at his insistence.

"Check on them steers. That's my job."

"White men are so dumb." She shook her head in dismay. "They make much work. When the buffalo were here, we only had to ride out and kill them for our food."

"Yeah, but the white man's got to own everything. He wants his brand on everything, like land and cattle and horses."

"You can't own the land." She looked at him in dismay. "This sagebrush is not yours or mine. It belongs to the spirits and everyone."

"I can see you don't know Old Man Crawford," he said, and laughed out loud, imagining this strong-minded woman and that bowlegged Texas rancher with his bilious white mustache standing toe to toe arguing about owning and not owning things. He could see Crawford in his knee-high handmade boots, big white hat, wearing that old leather beaded jacket he'd bought off some old squaw who claimed that Custer had worn it at the Big Horn. The old man would shout that she didn't know a damn thing about the ways of this world, and she would come right back at him with her hands on her hips firing her arguments just as strong as he did. It would be a sight to behold and remember.

"Are you sorry you came after me?" she asked, looking ahead.

"Does a bear sleep in the forest?" he asked, rubbing his clean-shaven upper lip on the side of his hand to heal an itch.

"Sometimes," she said, not sounding satisfied with his answer.

"I had to get the old man's horses back anyway. But I kinda missed your cooking." Something moved in the corner of his eye after he caught Eagle looking off in the easterly direction. He jerked out the Winchester, and she frowned at his action.

"I just spotted a fat-looking mule deer. We'll need the meat."

She agreed, and he trotted Eagle off in the direction the buck had moved. He topped the rise, and the deer raised his head to view this intruder in his land. The stag's reactions proved too slow, and the fast-moving 44/40 bullet struck him in the heart. He made a high jump in the air, then five or six hops before he crumbled into the sage. Slocum rose in the stirrups and waved Yellow Doe over with the rifle raised high. They had camp meat and a job to do.

By mid-afternoon the wind had come up waving the tall grass. They stopped at a stream to wash off the carcass and their dried hands stiff with blood. The rusty remains came off their skin hard as the V-shaped blue carcass of the deer remained sunk with rocks in the water to cool out. Only the stubs of the animal's legs parted the current in the pool as they bent over knee-deep in the creek and lathered their hands.

"Can we make your lodge tonight?" she asked, raising up.

"No, we're too far away to make it tonight and we've wasted too much time with the deer."

"You could have said I was too slow."

"No." He shook his head and leaned over to flush the soap off his fingers. "I was not displeased with your work." Without a towel, he began to dry his hands, using the front of his pants for that purpose, then reached up and reset his hat on his head to keep it from being blown away.

"Good," she said, sounding satisfied with his answer, and busied herself lathering her own hands and straightening up. As she stood with her bare shapely legs set apart in the swift water, the hem of her blouse rode on her hips. He drew in a deep breath at the thought of her fury in bed.

"Do you smell smoke?" he asked. He tested the wind for it. Nothing drove dread faster into his heart, or that of any experienced plainsman, than a prairie fire. The lye stink of a fire hung in the air, masking the eternal sweet grass and sage odors of the Powder River basin.

"Yes. What should we do?" Her face showed concern.

"I'm going to ride out and see if it's a grass fire. You stay here. We may need to pick up and ride whether that deer is cooled out or not. On this kind of a wind, the damn thing could even jump this creek." He rushed through the water for the bank to dry his feet, roll down his pants, pull on his boots, and go see about the fire.

He short-loped Eagle, standing in the stirrups. A prairie fire could outrun a horse on such a wind as whipped by his face. One had to be ready to ride to avoid such a fire. The small moisture of the snow was gone. Still, he could not see the smoke he'd expected, and pushed the gray on east to a higher point.

Ravens were yipping somewhere close by, over the wind's whistle. They must be fighting over a dead cow or something. Maybe challenging an eagle or a hawk. He could hear their yelps as he pushed Eagle up the slope hoping to discover the source of the smoke.

He blinked. There were three wagons, one on fire. He could see an ox had been filled with arrows and lay dying in its yoke. The yelping wasn't ravens or magpies at all, but a half-dozen bucks on painted ponies making charges at the beleaguered travelers huddled in the under the conveyances.

Slocum could do nothing else. He drew out his Winchester, let out the loudest cry he could find, and screaming like a wild man, charged Eagle off the hill. Either he buffaloed the bucks away and they took tail and ran, or they bunched up like dog soldiers, stood their ground, and held him off.

He was glad when they had a quick powwow on horseback and then turned tail. Whipping their ponies, they tore off to the northeast at breakneck speed. In an effort to keep them going, he rose in the stirrups and shot his rifle after them. There was no chance he'd hit any of them, but it did keep them moving. A volley of shots, the first he'd heard, came from the cheering wagon folks to add to his rout of the war party.

"Whew, mister. You're a sight for sore eyes," a gray-bearded straight-backed man said as he came out carrying a muzzle-loading Hawkins rifle.

"None of you have repeaters?" he asked in dismay as he dismounted.

"Nope, but we got two of them red devils. My name's Bob Mayfield," the man said. "You sure saved our hides today." A cheer went up from the others. He wasn't noticing the menfolks, but rather the sweet-looking gal in her twenties who stepped out from behind the wagon sucking on a blade of grass with a dress too short for a grown woman and lots of tanned leg showing. Her green eyes met his and he nodded, then turned back to Mayfield.

"You all better get that fire on that wagon put out," Slocum said, indicating the smoldering wagon tarp. Everyone, men and women, turned to the task.

"Gunpowder started it," Mayfield explained. "You ain't got an ox you'd sell us? They killed one of ours."

"I could sell you a steer, but he wouldn't be broken to work."

"We could train him." The man acted as if even one would be enough. "When could you bring him and how much?"

"Old Man Crawford is expecting to get fifty dollars a head for them this fall. I could bring one of them to you for that." He waited for the man's reply as the others finished dousing the burning canvas.

"I can rake up the money," the man finally said. "When will you have him here?"

"Day after tomorrow."

"Best you can do, I guess. Is there water nearby?" Mayfield asked, pulling on his earlobe.

"Due north a mile or so," Slocum said, not wanting to share his camp for the night with this lot of obvious homesteaders. Selling them one of Crawford's steers for an ox was good business, but not sharing a camp with them.

"I never caught your name," Mayfield said.

"Slocum. See you in two days." His gaze went to the girl in the short dress. She smiled slowly at him. There was something about her. She obviously did not have a man in the lot. She also knew her power to attract a man's gaze—something about the look in her eyes. He shook his head to dismiss her.

"You're from the South, ain't yeah, Slocum?"

"Texas," he lied. No need to give the man his life history, and besides, he had been in the Lone Star State enough since the war that he considered it more home than his native Georgia.

"We're all from Arkansas here. We're sure obliged for your help running off them red devils. See yeah in two days." Mayfield and the others waved. The girl in the short dress just smiled as she stretched and then hugged the wagon wheel's rim.

He let Eagle lope. He hoped the farmers managed to keep their guard up while he was gone. Then a shiver of disgust ran up his spine and shook his shoulders. They had already started coming to Wyoming. The sodbusters and land grabbers like Mayfield. He wondered what the girl's name was. Then he gouged Eagle in the sides with his spurs and sent him racing as he tried to wipe the image of the farmer's daughter out of his mind.

8

He remembered some part-shorthorn steers that stayed not far from his cow camp. The next evening back at the cow camp, he worked over a stiff sixty-foot reata. His purpose was to have two good lariats on his saddle to use to catch a steer. He needed a heeler to rope the animal's back feet if he'd really wanted to capture a full-blood longhorn or bust him a few times to get him to lead. But a roan cross would be less wild by his breeding, he finally decided.

"You're going to catch a steer for these farmers?" she asked, busy washing dishes in a deep pan.

She talked a lot for an Indian. He'd been married to one for a year when he had scouted for Major Mc-Kensie's outfit. Her name was Cutter, and all she ever said when he got back from a two-month scout and rode up was, "Your dick hard? Good." Then, before he could even answer her, she ducked her head, went in the lodge ahead of him, and undressed.

"Yes, the renegades killed one of their oxen," he said to Doe.

"Did you see the braves?"

"I only saw their butts going over the hill when I rode up shooting."

"It was not Long Knife's band." She shook her head to dismiss the idea.

"What do they look like? These had some long-tailed colored ponies. These had mostly bows and arrows and lances, or they'd have done more damage to them honyockers. And if them farmers had had good repeaters, they'd never got that close to them either."

"Long Knife has many rifles like yours and he rides good horses." She drew her shoulders back and, hands dripping suds, she shoved her breasts against the buckskin blouse's material.

"Since the army is right on his moccasin tracks and hard after him," he said, "the whole bunch of them are maybe starving up in those mountains too."

She shook her head in disbelief.

"How do you know they aren't starving up there?" he asked "The army ran Sitting Bull into Canada."

"Long Knife is my brother."

"Oh," he said as if that would make a lot of difference. That was who she was planning to join when he found her. He was probably the same one who had raided that ranch and given the army the slip in the Bighorns.

"I will go with you tomorrow to catch that steer."

"What do you know about roping?" he asked, not looking up from his job of flexing the stiff-braided lariat.

"You will see." She dried her hands and then moved beside him, close enough that even with the heat and odor of the campfire he could smell her musk. She rested her head on his shoulder, and then she reached in his lap and tested him. With a grin, she wrinkled her broken nose at him as she looked him eye to eye.

"It is time we did better things than worked ropes."

"I agree," he said, looking hard at the highlights of the fire's flames dancing in her brown pupils. He put the rope aside and went inside the tent after her.

• • •

Before breakfast the next morning, he saddled two horses, taking a long-bodied bay for his mount. The boys called brown gelding Rough because he broke loose and pitched on most cold mornings, but he was the best horse in the bunch to go past a steer after you roped one to trip him. He was Old Man Crawford's favorite tripping horse, and Slocum was proud the rustlers hadn't gotten away with him. He saddled Brownie for Yellow Doe.

Cold-backed, Rough acted snorty when Slocum cinched down his tack, and Slocum tried to recall when he'd ridden the bay last. He liked the gray and Brownie, but maybe he'd passed this one up too often. But it didn't make a lot of difference. Slocum had time to ride him around close and settle him down before they started out. Yellow Doe would not have their breakfast ready for a while, and he'd kind of take the slack out of this gelding in the meantime.

He rechecked the latigoes with his fingers and made sure they were pulled up tight. If this horse thought he was a bucker, then Slocum wanted his rig on solid enough that he didn't end up on the belly side after the second jump. He took the cheek strap of the bridle in his left hand, and then swung up as the pony circled into his hand.

His boot toe found the right stirrup and was in place before he let the horse have his head. Rough bogged his ears out of sight in the gray morning light, and grunting like a big shoat, left out bucking across the prairie.

Slocum fought to jerk his head up. No use. The horse was simply getting up his speed and diving higher. While his style of sky-hopping wasn't threatening to unseat his rider, he sure was persistent from Slocum's perspective. He began to spur the horse. If he couldn't make him quit, then he'd simply wear him out. That became his new theory. He began to whip and charge the crow-hopping devil between his knees.

The horse issued the most awful sounds, like a pig

caught under a gate in protest, and soon quit. He stopped, standing straddle-legged over a sagebush, and blew as if he'd run a mile. As cautiously as he could, Slocum lifted the reins and touched the horse lightly on the side with his outside spur not wanting the ride to be over. Then, after what seemed like a long time, Rough dropped his head, gave a loud blow, and headed back for camp.

Slocum could see Yellow Doe in the distance, using her hand to shield the rising sun and looking for him. He waved at her to say he was all right as the horse, with his head dropped down, set off in an easy single-foot trot. Good thing that was over, Slocum decided, and set in for the quarter-mile ride and one of her hearty breakfasts to separate his navel from his backbone at the other end.

Later, they found the small band he called the barn bunch grazing in a long swale. Undaunted by the appearance of two riders, the red-white steers barely lifted their heads. Slocum shook out a loop and motioned for Yellow Doe to ride to that side. Out of habit, he threw a John Blocker-style loop, so called because of a famous cattle dealer who used most of his rope making a loop. Slocum was using the regular reata that he carried in case he needed to pull a steer out of a bog or to treat one.

"I don't catch one with this one, you give me yours," he said to her as she undid her stiffer one.

She nodded. Her bare legs shined in the sun as she guided Brownie more with her knees than the reins. A well-broken horse would do that, so Slocum didn't figure she was ruining him. All the time they were traveling down the wide grassy depression after the cattle.

He gave Rough the boot to charge after the steer, and all hell broke loose. The bay wasn't crow-hopping this round, he was having himself a wall-eyed fit, and Slocum was wishing that those breeds had eaten him. Rough sunfished his belly up to the sun, landed, and then dove in the sky off his hind legs. Next he hit on all

fours, then jumped sideways. Slocum lost the right stirrup, and despite his whipping the horse over the head
and ears with the reins, nothing could discourage
Rough's bucking and hog-grunting.

Then, after a flying trip to the moon, Slocum found
himself in a pile between two clumps of sage. On his
butt, he watched the pony still bucking and diving high
enough that he could look up and see the cinches from
where he sat. Damn, he would teach that old pony some
new tricks.

"This steer good enough for those *Ha-yonkers*?" she
asked, dragging a reluctant two-year-old roan up on the
end of her lariat.

"Hon-yockers!" he said to correct her, getting up and
dusting off his pants with his hat. "It will do fine. Now
all Brownie has to do is carry us double back to camp
and drag that critter too."

"I will walk."

"Hell, no, you won't. You came horseback, you go
back horseback. Besides, the old man owes you something for cowboying this morning." He swung up behind her and lifted the rope up over his leg.

With his arm around her waist and crowded up against
the cantle behind her, he was pleased at this new turn
of events. He clucked for Brownie and booted him to
go. The bay horse might have been gentle and he might
have been his favorite horse, but riding him double must
not have suited that cow pony's fancy for he began to
buck, dragging the bellowing steer on the end of the
reata along behind.

They both bailed off to save a wreck, and then they
both lay on the ground laughing until Slocum's belly
hurt. Tears ran down her face. Back on their feet, he
kissed her, then dusted her off as the gelding and steer
went out of sight. Brownie took the fast-tied steer back
to camp long before Slocum and Yellow Doe walked in.

A damn good thing for him that those Texas cowboys
would never know the truth about the sale of the roan
steer. Life was too short for that kind of ribbing.

The next day, by himself, he delivered the future ox to Mayfield's camp. The critter led good on the end of a lariat after all his training the day before, and Mayfield acted impressed with his choice. He paid Slocum off with a sack of coins and paper money, but it all looked real enough to suit him.

"Have some lunch with us," Mayfield said.

"I could stand some coffee," Slocum said, his mouth dry from the ride over.

"Come on then," the man said, and Slocum hitched the gray horse to a wagon wheel.

They sat down with the other men on some narrow board benches, and the women in long calico dresses served them plates of food. He wondered where the gal he'd seen in the short dress was at, and didn't have long to wait to find out.

"Here you are, Mr. Slocum," she said, and delivered him a full platter of steaming stew and yellow corn bread.

"Coffee is all he needs now," Mayfield said between spoonfuls to the girl.

"Thank you, ma'am," Slocum said. "I'd be a plumb fool to turn down such fine food."

"You use cow in your coffee?" she asked.

"Not if I can keep him from stepping in it," he said, looking into her green eyes. She was shorter than he thought, but she was no child either.

His reply made the men all laugh and nod in approval.

"I meant milk. Or sugar?" she asked.

"Just coffee will be fine."

"I'll get you a cup." She turned on her heels.

"I guess you figured out by now. She's different than most women," Mayfield said privately with an elbow in Slocum's side to keep his attention. The bobbing of heads of the others reinforced the man's soft words. "She's a witch. Already in her young life she's lost two husbands. Knew when each of them would die and couldn't save them."

"I'll keep that in mind," Slocum said soberly. He

knew something was wrong, but a witch? That made more sense to him as he considered her. He planned to avoid her spell. The food didn't taste poisoned when he tried it, but there was still that coffee she'd gone after.

"Did her husbands use cream in their coffee?" he asked Mayfield under his breath.

"I don't know. Why?"

"Nothing," Slocum said, wondering if he had anything in common with them as he enjoyed the slice of fresh-made corn bread. It had been years since he'd had any this tasty.

"Here's your coffee."

He looked up, thanked her, and then took the cup. In her green cat eyes he saw the power, and wondered when their paths would cross again. Maybe never—no, she knew his skills and if she needed him again, she would draw him in. The skin under his collar crawled at the notion of her power.

"We're still grateful to you for running off those Injuns for us," she said. Despite the sun's heat, he felt cold when she smiled at him and made a little bow.

He looked around to see how many were looking at them, feeling embarrassed at the attention she had given him. The rest of those honyockers needed to be aware she probably was the one who had sent up the smoke to find him. And it had been a damn little fire too, hardly more than scorching one of the tall ribs of the wagon, he noticed now as he savored bites of the food. He would be glad to be gone from these folks' camp and from her. One thing he knew for certain, the reason he'd been glad they had not camped by him the day before: There was a witch among them. There were good witches and bad witches, but as far as he was concerned, they all should be avoided.

9

To study their tracks, he dropped off his horse in the slanting rays of late afternoon. They were far to the south of his range. He and Doe had left camp with a packhorse before daylight, and throughout the day had cut several signs of cattle moving south. He could almost imagine those black rogues heading back for the live oak of the country of their birth. Chances were those mossy horns knew that they came from the south and that this was the way home. Animal instinct must be pushing them. There were no horse prints mixed with cattle sign, except for those of a passing band of mustangs who raised their heads from grazing when Slocum and Yellow Doe rode by. Those bronc cattle were plain drifting out of the country, Slocum decided, and he mounted up again.

"We'll have to sleep out here under the stars tonight," he said to warn her of his intention to remain on their tracks until he found the cattle.

"Fine," she said, squinting against the low sun in the west that threatened to fall behind the Bighorns. "But we should find a place soon."

"I agree. There's a line of cottonwoods, must be water there, and those steers can't be far either. All this sign I see is fresh."

She agreed, and they loped off in the direction of the green treetops under the blood-red sunset. He turned in the saddle and looked over their back trail—nothing. Maybe in another day's riding they could find the strays and then head back to camp. He hoped so.

From horseback, he dragged in a few logs on the end of his lariat for her to burn as twilight settled on the land. He watched her cross the ground to get something from a pannier she'd taken off the packhorse. He admired how she always moved like a deer, jumping over a downed limb as if it was nothing, her actions always precise and quick when she prepared meals or did any work. Meanwhile, he unsaddled their horses, hobbled the three of them, then headed for camp dragging both rigs. He piled them close by the fire where he figured that they'd both sleep, and sat down on his haunches as she poured him a cup of fresh coffee.

"Do you miss your people?" he asked, looking over his coffee vapors and considering the orange-red sky in the west.

"I miss the camp life. There were people who could make you laugh, who told funny stories, and ones who told you history of our people. There were some who worked magic and medicine. But now that the spirit has left us, it would not be the same." She shook her head as she stirred the frying potatoes. "Without the Great Spirit, there is nothing to go back for."

"The Great Spirit left? Why?" He frowned at her words, pausing before sipping his coffee.

"The spirit is gone. Death is in my people's eyes. I do not want to look into them."

Nodding some, he considered her explanation. Settled cross-legged on the ground, he dragged out one of the few remaining small cigars from his shirt pocket and lighted it with a stick from the campfire.

"Maybe the problem is you," he said after drawing

in the sweet smoke and letting the vapors bathe his lungs and settle him.

"Me?" She blinked, looking back at him.

"Spirits are inside people or they aren't. Maybe you let yours escape."

She nodded and looked off in the night as some coyotes began to howl. "How can you—a white man—know that?"

"Makes sense to me. I have known spirits. They have delivered me from some serious places when I needed them to. When I believed in them they always worked the best."

"My home is not up there, in the land of the Queen where Sitting Bull hides behind her skirt." She motioned to the North Star in the darkening sky. "There is no spirit in those camps."

"Is there a home hiding like hunted dogs in the Bighorns where the snow gets deeper than a man's head in winter?"

"I don't know, but—some day I must go there and see for myself."

"When you must go, go. You may take a horse or those two mustangs I took from Deveau. But don't tell me when you plan to leave," he said, and looked away, feeling a large rock forming in his stomach at the thought of losing her. At last he knew the truth about his future; before the old man came back, he would be alone again in the cow camp.

"Eat," she said, and shoved a plate of food at him. "I have not gone yet. Don't act so sad. You may wish for me to leave before I go."

"I doubt that." He studied the plate of browned potatoes and chunks of cooked deer she'd brought along.

"We will see." She poured him more coffee in his cup, then filled her own plate, and they sat back to listen to the wails of the coyotes in the growing darkness.

The next day, they met the sun in the saddles, leading their packhorse and filing down into a long deep valley lined with sheer rock walls shaped like organ pipes and covered in pines. He had searched several times from the tops of the outcroppings for any signs of cattle or anything, and had seen little below. Still, the tracks led in, so they followed. The trail they rode forced them to go single file.

"See that smoke?" He pointed.

"Yes," she said from behind.

"You stay back, I'll go check on it. Could be a settler or an outlaw den." He turned in the saddle to look for her reply.

Her nod was good enough. He hurried the gray down the trail, anxious to see who was there and if his strays were in the area.

At the bottom, he drew the saddle gun out, levered a shell in, and sent Eagle charging down the valley of pines. The smoke was ahead when he spotted the hide staked on the ground flesh side up. There was no mistaking the tail attached—it was a black longhorn's bush. He searched around, stepping down with the Winchester ready.

His breath was on fire. Damn rustlers. He'd string them up. *This job keeps getting tougher, old man.* But they'd slaughtered a V Bar C critter and it was his job to avenge it. The gauntlet was down. Where in hell had they gone? He caught the gray, swung up, and bent low in the saddle as they swept under the boughs. Their camp must be right ahead.

Then he heard the screams as he pushed into their camp. Naked brown children ran down the valley, and half-dressed women who'd been busy jerking the meat scrambled to their feet at the sight of him and raced away in panic. Their wails disoriented him as he drew in his horse to a sliding stop, expecting an arrow in his back any moment.

A crippled woman with only a filthy rag tied around her waist pulled herself along on the ground. Her stringy hair was matted and her hollow dark eyes looked at him as if he would surely be her executioner. She held up filthy blood-dried hands to protect her head, and cowered and whimpered like a kicked dog.

"Are there no men here?" he demanded.

Doe's sharp words were in Sioux as she ran past him. Her appearance and words drew tears of relief on the woman's face. Still cowering the woman mumbled something back to her.

"All the men have been gone for two weeks," Doe said, translating the woman's words. "They fear that they are all dead."

"Gather them up and tell them I won't kill them," he said in disgust over the situation. "Crawford can afford a couple steers if they're starving." He emptied the rifle chamber and held the next cartridge down so the rifle was empty before he slammed the Winchester back in the scabbard.

"They only killed one," she said after him.

"That won't be enough," he said. "I'm going to round up the rest and head them up the mountain. I'll drop another for these people to eat. Tell them to bring their knives to the foot of the mountain. I want the rest of the cattle headed uphill before I shoot it. Otherwise they might scatter and it will take us a day to round them up."

"What will this old man say?" she asked with a concerned frown on her forehead.

"I'll say wolves got them."

"Yes. They are like wolves," she agreed, walking beside him as he checked the gray to a walk. He didn't want to look at any more of the naked, defeated inhabitants of the camp. Never before had he ever seen a band of the Plains Indians in such distress. His shoulders shook at the picture of the starving woman with her dried-up babes in filthy rags.

"Lots of damn wolves out here," he said, and then headed the gray down the valley at a long lope.

He swept around the eight head grazing in a grassy hammock. His approach sent them flying back along the base of the mountain. Satisfied they were going his way, he fell in on their heels. As they drew closer to the trail, he shook loose his reata and built a loop. They knew how they had come down, and animals usually made tracks back the same way when driven.

A jet-black three-year-old with his brown tail stuck high in the air was leading the bunch, probably the ringleader of the strays. He would take them back to their home range, which was just what Slocum wanted. A potbellied brown steer trailed the lot, and when the black leader struck the trail, several of the others lost their footing in the panic and fell backwards.

He reined up in time not to panic them while they scrambled to their feet. As they milled around, he could see the leader was a hundred feet up and still moving on the narrow ledge. Another of the blacks paused to horn the brown one back to subjugate him, and the smaller steer broke away to escape the sharp horn tips.

It was the chance Slocum needed. He rushed in and swung the loop. The great O settled over the steer's horns and Slocum dallied hard, setting the gray down. His reata stretched tight as it wrapped around the horn, and Slocum held it back in his right hand as he glanced at the mountain. The others were not slowing down in their escape. Good. They would be heading in the right direction. He turned back to the captured steer on the end of his lariat.

He hitched the rope around a pine tree, and the bucking, bawling steer on the end moved away at his approach. Using his spur, Slocum moved the gray in closer for a shot. Satisfied with the range, he drew out the .31 and shot the steer in the center of the forehead. The scrubby longhorn fell in a pile, and out of nowhere three screaming Indian woman ran in with their knives flashing in the sun.

For a moment he wondered about his rope's safety. But one of the women, wearing only a short rag from a wagon sheet for a skirt, expertly coiled it up and walked toward him.

"The spirits be with you," she said, and handed him

the reata in a tight coil. Her features were sharp, her face so drawn over her cheekbones that her skin looked like sun-cured rawhide. Her breasts had dried up to small saucers on her thin chest. She was young, maybe younger than Doe.

"And with you," he said, busy tying the reata on with the leather saddle string. He was grateful when she walked back to help the others, who were already feasting on the steer's raw liver and organs. Some of the children, after hesitating in the pines, were unable to resist any longer and rushed in to join the feeding. The copper smell of blood and unwashed bodies filled his nose and renewed the bile rising up his throat.

"I want to bring them back, those two mustangs that you said I could have," Doe said, riding up.

"Fine, but what will they do with them? Eat them?" he asked.

"No, they plan to move to the reservation with them. They will have enough jerky now to go there with this other steer you gave them."

"Do they know that it's a long ways to Dakota?" he asked, considering the many desolate miles between them and the Standing Rock Agency.

"They know."

"Good, you can have them." He booted his horse for the trail. He had steers to herd back to the home range. *Old man, you owed them those two head.*

He didn't want to have to look at the women and children again. As he rode, he tried to bring up thoughts of the old days. The stomp-dancing around the great fire, the deep drums' thunder in the night, shrill singing, chanting, and eagle-bone whistles cutting the night's darkness beyond. Squaws dressed in elk skin flirting with him from behind their colorful wool trade blankets wrapped around their subtle forms. The diamond glint in their eyes as they winked their long dark lashes and then swished suggestively away, knowing he was bound to follow one of them beyond the campfire into the shadows of the towering tepees.

Once he was in the maize, a sharp whistle would get him to look her way, and then a curled finger would invite him inside the flap. He'd leave his rifle outside and remove his hat, ducking to enter the warmth of her tepee. There she would kneel naked in the orange glow of the fire pit. Her unblemished skin would be as sleek as a grain-fed pony. Long black hair shaken loose would hide her proud breasts, and under the muscled rolls of her flat belly he would see the black V between her copper legs. The thought of those gates of paradise now caused a stirring in his pants that strained against the leather.

He spurred the gray up the hill and when he looked back, she came with the packhorse. Her long braids were bobbing in the wind. Her people had lived in this land like the once-plentiful buffalo. Now their spirit was gone.

10

By the first light, he saddled Brownie for her. She rushed about camp making sure she had everything to take with her when she delivered the pair of mustangs to the women. Finally, with her fancy trade blankets tied in a bundle for a bedroll, she busied herself strapping them on behind the cantle. He drew his last cigar out and lighted it as she added a portion of the deer jerky she'd made to the saddlebags.

He drew in the sweet smoke, then spat on the lucifer match so it wouldn't ignite something, and threw it down. The fresh wind swept his shaven face. Brownie stomped around impatient to be on his way. Slocum dropped on his haunches and watched Yellow Doe's legs flash under the fringed hem as she ran for something else from the pannier.

She returned with a supply of salt and held it before him. "They need this."

He agreed. Then, with a grin, she reached down and hugged his neck, spilling both of them on the ground. They both laughed aloud. Sitting up on his butt, he looked her in the face and shook his head. "I hadn't ought to let you go." He sighed deeply, and then drew the .31 out of his belt. "You better have this. It's loaded."

She nodded, took the revolver, and then pushed her mouth to his. The sweetness of her kiss fueled a fire inside him, and he knew if she didn't leave soon he would have to have her again.

"Go!" he said, twisting his mouth away. "Before I change my mind about you doing this alone."

"You go find those stray steers today, and I'll be back in your blankets tomorrow night." She stuck out a challenging bottom lip at him as she rose. Then she wrinkled her nose at him.

Pistol in her hand, she ran to where Brownie had trailed the reins and was busy grazing. In a bound, she was aboard the saddle, and rode by the corral to get the leads of the two shaggy mustangs. Sticking the gun in her saddlebags, she gave him a coyote war cry, bent low in the saddle, and then raced southward. The thick tails of the two painted ponies flagged high as they paced to keep up with Brownie's lope. In the purple orange light of dawn, Slocum drew on the cigar and a red ring glowed on the end. Then he let the smoke trail out his nose. *One more day in Eden had passed.*

By noontime, he had pushed far enough to the west to reach the small community called Mansford. Numerous steers had drifted in this direction, and he intended to replenish his supply of cigars and then drive them back. Besides smokes, he needed a sack of fresh flour and some hard candy as a gift for Yellow Doe.

He dismounted in front of the log store, wrapped the reins on the lodgepole rail, and noting some other saddled horses that were hobbled out in the jack pines, went inside.

The store's dark interior required a moment for his eyes to adjust. A couple of smoky lamps hung under the rafters, and he saw the flash of some eyes and faces looking in his direction from the bar to the left. The room reeked of dyes, tanned leather, smoked meat, whiskey, horse sweat, and stale tobacco, the usual odors of civilization in such places.

"What can I do for you?" the big man standing behind the counter asked.

"You have any small cigars?" Slocum asked, rubbing his lower lip in the side of his hand. He considered going over and getting a good shot of whiskey as he mentally went over his list.

"I have a box of them that just came in. I get twenty bucks for the whole box."

"A little rich for my blood. Better give me a fistful."

"Sure—"

"Don't sell that rebel sum-bitch a damn thing, Thurman!" It was Walter, one of the Jackson brothers, who strode over from the bar. "He needs to get the hell off our range." His brother Hansen came up beside him. No doubt fortified with whiskey, both of the portly figures looked heeled and ready.

Slocum could see the worked-up anger written on their full faces as they came under the light. Then, as they moved under the lamp, the dark shadow of their four-peak flat-brim hats covered their facial expressions. The danger of not seeing a man's facial features in time to draw could get a man killed, and Slocum was relieved when they came to the edge of the lamp ring and he could make them out again.

His gun. Damn. He'd even left the empty holster at camp. And earlier he'd given Yellow Doe the .31 that he'd carried in his waistband. The other Colt was outside in his saddlebags. He'd damn sure gotten lax as hell being around her.

"I'm not armed," he said in surrender, and raised his hands up about shirt-pocket high to show them.

"Get armed!" Walter tossed a Colt on the counter beside him. When the .44 stopped spinning, Slocum made no move for it, and instead looked back at them. It was probably his own handgun that they'd taken in the scuffle. He wasn't that big a fool. Even if he managed to reach it in time, chances were they had either jammed it or it was empty. With witnesses in the store, he had to make a move for the weapon. Otherwise shooting him would be plain murder. They hung folks for that. He'd take his chance on a bluff until something better came along.

"You yellow belly, go for it," Walter Jackson said, his hand ready to reach for the ivory handle in the holster at his side. Boastfully he bent forward and waved both hands, interlocking his fingers, then springing them free, daring Slocum to go for the Colt.

"Boys, I don't want no trouble in here," Thurman protested. The man raised his arms as if to wave them away.

"Ain't going to be none on my account, mister," Slocum said, not daring to look away from the Jacksons.

"You Jacksons back off now," the store owner warned.

"Thurman, we ain't backing down. He called us bastards," Walter said.

"I never heard it."

"Well, he did out there the other day, and we ain't taking that shit off no damn rebel scum that's up here stealing our grass."

Hansen nodded his head in agreement.

"Boys, I've got lots of things in here that don't need shot up," Thurman said with a fear-filled voice.

"You can charge it to his rich Texas boss. There's plenty of his cattle out there to cover the cost. Go for your gun or die!"

"What's going on in here?" the deputy Henry Clay asked, dressed in his black suit as he blocked the light coming in the open door.

Slocum breathed, not realizing how short of air he had become. Both of the twins turned to the door and swore in disgust. Clay crossed the room and frowned at Slocum, then back at the pair.

"What the hell's going on in here?" the deputy demanded again. "Better ask them," Slocum said, and turned to the counter. He picked up the .44 and opened the side gate. Then he spun the cylinder letting the two bullets fall out and clunk one at a time on the counter.

"They knew that wasn't loaded fully, didn't they?" Thurman asked under his breath.

"I need a box of .44 cartridges too," Slocum said, ignoring Clay's dressing down of the twins.

"I guess you're taking the gun too?" Thurman said.

"Yeah," Slocum said. "You heard them give it back to me." The storekeeper nodded as he set the box of bullets on the counter.

"What's your side of this?" Clay asked Slocum.

"I come in for a few cigars." He turned to Thurman. "And flour and a sack of hard candy too."

"You seem to make them mad every time your trails cross," the deputy said, looking vexed.

"I can't help it. They have a burr under their saddle. When Old Man Crawford comes this fall, they can bitch at him about using their range. Those are his steers out there. But I'm willing to bet that they ain't got any title nor deed to it, least not one I've seen."

"It's free range. I guess that you're right. But I don't need any killing in my district either, do you understand?"

"Why are you looking at me?" Slocum demanded as he counted out the money to Thurman. Then he stuck the empty .44 in his waistband.

" 'Cause I figure when push comes to shove them two are babies at that game."

"You've got the wrong man, Clay." Slocum shook his head, turning to face him.

"No, I haven't. You aren't some simple ranch hand or green kid left all summer to tend cows. I don't figure a man rich enough to own five hundred steers is dumb enough to let a fool watch after that much money in one wad."

"You through?" Slocum gathered his purchases in his arm.

"I'm through, but I'm warning both you and them,

I'm not letting you have a range war up here.''

"Then you better tie them up good. They're using up a helluva lot of my patience.''

"Slocum, you better mind my words,'' Clay said after him as he stepped outside the store with his goods in his arms and drew a breath of fresh air tinged with sage and pine fragrance. He felt the muscles in his shoulders loosen when he laid the sack of flour over the saddle seat. Then he put the shells, sacks of candy, and smokes in his saddlebags.

His fingers fumbled with the leather latigoes, cinching them up tight with effort. He didn't glance back to the doorway, knowing the deputy blocked it. Once he reached the horizon he knew he'd feel a lot more secure.

He swung up balancing the cotton sack of flour in his lap. Bent over the horn, he touched his hat for Clay peering out the doorway, swung Eagle around, and rode east at a short lope. *Damn, old man, this job gets tougher and tougher.*

11

He listened to the coyote's mournful cry and watched the moon rise. Still no sign of Doe. Finally he tossed out the last of his coffee and then, niggled by her failure to return as she promised, crawled between his soagans, which he'd dragged outside the tent. Lying on his back, he studied the stars overhead wondering what had detained her. In two days' herding, he had gathered most of the strays and driven them back to their range.

Maybe she had left for her own people in the Bighorns. He had made her promise him not to tell whenever she was leaving him. This was his own fault. He rolled over on his arm for a pillow and drew in a deep breath that cut him in the lungs. It wasn't the sage-scented air that knifed him. It was knowing that he didn't have her muscular ripe body to tussle with, that she wasn't there to hug him at night and press her nipples in his bare back. To reach over, fondle and tease him with her nimble fingers until he was forced to turn back and settle the matter.

Then a coyote vented his sorrow in a long mournful

wail to the quarter moon. Slocum closed his eyes, not to the sound, but to his loss. He drifted in and out of sleep until he gave up trying. Stiff and fatigued, he made coffee and waited for sunup. By damn, he'd go find her.

At dawn, he saddled Eagle and rode south. Crossing the rolling grass sea at mid-morning, he spotted the black steers. They were staying around close for a change. Good. He trotted the gray. Each time he topped a rise he hoped to catch sight of her, but instead he saw herds of antelope and jackrabbits, and flushed up a few prairie chickens in a thundering burst of wings.

He dropped into the canyon of the pines in late afternoon. The hoofprints in the dust didn't tell him much as he rode down the face of the mountain. Nor could he see any activity in the valley as he leaned over and scanned the canyon floor. What had happened to her? She'd had two days' head start. Had she gone to the Bighorns or headed for Standing Rock reservation with the ragged band of women and children?

He found traces of the band's camp. Then he saw the prints of the shod horses all over the campground. His heart stopped. They were military shoes. He'd know them anywhere. Damn. The army had found the band and had taken her with them. They would be headed for Standing Rock for certain. He sat on his haunches whipping his leg with the reins and wondering how to recover her.

He should have accompanied her. The damn steers would have been there when he got back. What should he do? He drew his upper front teeth over his dried lower lip and fretted over his options. The soldiers couldn't travel fast herding that many women and children. He looked to the east. They would probably hold them at the army's temporary camp on the Powder River crossing and wait for wagons to haul them. Back in the spring, he and the old man had stopped there to talk to some shavetail lieutenant whose small supply company was waiting for the return of a troop out looking for renegades.

That would be a good day's ride to the northeast. He checked his cinch, swung up, and set the gray eastward. No good would come of the army herding those women and children. Cattle received better care in most instances. Too much bitterness remained toward the Sioux among the enlisted men over the Big Horn battle and Custer's demise. He needed to hurry. They'd better not harm a hair on her head.

With a glance back at the sun low in the west, he realized that daylight only had a few more hours. He shifted the familiar weight of the .44 to the side in the holster and urged Eagle on faster.

He got a few hours' sleep wrapped in a blanket during the night, and then was up and moving again. He used the silver light of the moon to guide him northeast through the low sagebrush; the tracks were no trouble to follow.

At dawn, his mouth dry, he spotted the scattered cottonwoods that lined the Powder. He tried to see a campfire or any sign, but there was nothing except for the long haunting shadows of the rustling trees and the ripple of the stream. They were still ahead of him.

After a drink and letting the gray have his fill, he followed the river trail and worked his way northward. By sunup he spotted their encampment. There was a lot of dust as the soldiers caught and saddled their horses. In a guarded circle, he could see the captive women and children seated on the ground. There was no sign of Doe, but he felt confident that she was there.

Then he saw a tall figure, clad in buckskin, leaning on a rifle. The sun shone on his shoulder-length red hair. The buckskinner seemed to be observing all the activities. Slocum recognized the legendary Whipper Murdock. Murdock's explosive temper was well known on the frontier, and Slocum knew from his own past experience dealing with the man not to turn his back on him either. He must be scouting for the soldiers. Slocum pushed the gray down the slope on an angle to intersect with the scout.

Using the long-barrel Sharps to lean on, the red-bearded man turned and looked him over mildly when Slocum rode up.

"Morning, Texas," the man said, then turned back as if concerned about something else.

"Morning," Slocum said, wondering what held the big man's interest.

"That damn squaw of mine better get up here with my grub or she's getting the hiding of her life," Murdock said.

"Sioux?" Slocum asked, knowing in his heart who the man spoke about.

"Yeah, the bitch! I bought her fair and square from her father and she's run off with a damn French breed once, but I've got her back this time and she'll learn to mind me or else." He shook his head in disapproval. "You Texans don't know nothing about Injun women."

"I reckon not. Guess you've fought a lot of them?"

"This bunch here put up a helluva fight two days ago when we jumped their camp. We killed all the bucks. Must have been twenty-five. Then we gathered up all their sluts and spawn," Murdock lied.

Slocum saw her coming from the camp. Her fringe whipped in the wind as she carried a plate of food. She hesitated for a moment at the sight of him, but quickly recovered as if he did not exist. No need to risk her being hurt in a scuffle with Murdock. Besides, the army would take their scout's side, and Slocum was outnumbered. He drew his breath and tried to think of a way.

"Gawdamn took you long enough." Murdock growled.

She gave him the plate and dropped her gaze. Slocum swung back up on his horse. He noticed that Murdock had handed her the long rifle to hold while he spooned the food in his mouth, a portion of it running down his long auburn whiskers.

"You haven't seen a saddle and a bay horse carrying a V bar C brand, have you?" Slocum asked. It would be pure suicide for both of them for him to try to take her away from him at this point. But he had no intention of leaving her with this red-bearded lying billy goat who'd once sold her to Deveau.

Murdock blinked his eyes and stopped shoveling in the beans "Why?" he asked with his mouth full.

"A bay horse was stolen from my cow camp."

"It was contraband. I found it and I'm claiming it." He gave Slocum a grim look, and then went back to eating as if the matter was settled for his part.

"It belongs to Old Man Crawford and I'm claiming it for him."

Murdock raised his great barrel chest under the dirty leather shirt, and a scowl formed on his face as if he considered the words a personal affront.

Slocum watched the man carefully for any move or threat as he dried his right palm on his pants leg. It still wasn't the time to kill this loudmouth pig, not with him a military scout and in an army camp, though the urge was strong to fight back.

"You look familiar to me. What the hell is your name?" the scout demanded. He closed his left eye and peered at Slocum with his right one.

"Slocum."

"I ain't placed you." He waved the great spoon around as if to reach out and connect the name and times past together. "But that bay horse is mine now, so you just ride on, cowboy." He waved him off with the utensil.

"I guess the officer in charge can decide," Slocum said.

"You want your ass blown off?" The scout closed his left eye to stare at him.

"You aren't going to do that in front of all these witnesses," Slocum said, and rode off, feeling twinges in his back muscles as he headed for the camp's center. He wished he could do something about Yellow Doe's situation, but for the moment she would be considered a captive by the military, and that would mean taking on Murdock and the army. Better to bring up the stolen horse first. He could get the feel of the outfit and what his chances of taking her out of there might be.

"Good morning," the gray-sideburned officer with the silver bars on his shoulder said, striding over to greet him.

"Captain," Slocum said, and dismounted.

"What can I do for you, sir?"

"Slocum's my name and I represent the V Bar C ranch."

"My name's Landers." The man drew off his glove and they shook hands. "You don't have some cattle to sell, do you?" he asked. "We're going to be very short on meat at our camp at the ford with the addition of the many hostiles we've captured."

"I could sell you some steers. But my business here today is recovering a bay horse that was stolen from our cow camp."

"There was a cow pony in their possession. A bay, but I think that—"

"I've already heard that your scout Mr. Murdock claims it as contraband." He tossed his head in that direction.

"Yes." The officer looked off to where Murdock and Doe stood on the side of the hill as if considering the matter. "But if you are a legal representative of the brand owner, then the horse and gear will be returned to you."

"I have a letter in my saddlebags." Slocum offered to go for it.

"No need. Sergeant O'Reilly! Go get the saddle and bay horse for Mr. Slocum."

"Sir, he's—" the big lantern jawed noncom began with some dread in his loud voice.

"I know who claims him. Who's running this man's army, us or Murdock?" the blue-eyed man demanded.

"By God, we do, sir." O'Reilly straightened to well over six feet.

"Then Sergeant, go get this man's horse and rig."

The stiff-backed noncom saluted, turned on his heel,

and marched across the camp, but not without drawing some concerned looks that Slocum noted from the busy recruits packing up to leave.

"Can you bring in ten head of cattle to our camp about ten miles north of here?" the captain asked.

"I can, but they'll cost you fifty dollars a head."

"Fair price, if they're fat. I can give you a draft on the army for the money if that's satisfactory."

"They're in good flesh. I guess the old man would take that." Slocum nodded, considering the sale as something the old man would approve.

"Captain!" Murdock shouted, and came down the hill trailed by Doe. "Don't be giving my property away to no damn worthless cowboy."

"I'll handle this," Landers said to Slocum, and stepped toward. "Murdock, this man is the legal owner."

"Then the gawdamn army owes me a hundred dollars to replace it. What in the hell's my squaw going to ride?"

"I'm not obligated to provide your or your wife's transportation."

"Wait till I talk to General Terry about this matter. I'll have your ass in such a sling you'll regret ever giving this damn puncher shit!" The anger in the man's face matched his beard.

"You threaten me, Murdock, and you'll find yourself in irons the rest of the tour." Though a short man, Landers didn't lack any authority when he spoke.

"Cowboy, I ever see your ass again, you're dead meat!" Murdock showed his yellow teeth between the parted red hair.

"Any time suits me," Slocum said, looking him square in the eye.

"Murdock, get to your scouting duties," Landers said.

His green pupils gleaming under the floppy brim, Murdock turned on his heels and jerked the rifle away from Doe. Then he gave her a ruthless shove aside that sent her reeling. It was all Slocum could do not to draw his .44 and gun the man down in his tracks.

"Your horse, sir," the big noncom said, handing him the reins.

He nodded and thanked the officer after promising him that he would drive the steers to his camp in two days. Doe looked back at him for a second, and then she shook her head no as she hurried after the scout.

The time wasn't right. He frowned, considering her signal. What did she mean? He held the reins of Brownie in his hands as he watched her half-run to keep up with the furious scout as he stomped through camp. He could almost hear the man's angry words over the loss of the bay that he offered to whoever might listen.

Slocum turned the gray and, with a heavy heart, started back. He'd get those cattle gathered and in the meantime figure a way to get her out of Murdock's clutches. Somehow he'd have do that. *Damn, old man, this summer has taken some hard twists.*

12

He let the long-strided Rough take his own lead to head them off as the steers broke to the left. On his way riding east, he'd gathered a dozen head to sell to the army. At this point, he'd not slept in so long that he couldn't recall having had any decent rest. It made him edgy, and when a long-eared jack shot out like a gunshot from under a sage bush, he almost drew his .44 and killed it.

In disgust, he finally reined up Rough and watched the steers head north on a high lope. There were others that he could cut out easier than those. His two favorite cow ponies needed a rest, so he had taken the long-bodied bay, and after a short episode of crow-hopping had lined Rough out for the Powder.

With his mind full of concern for Doe's well-being and how she was faring, he hardly noticed the next bunch of steers that lifted their heads at his approach. They acted less spooky than the first ones, and he set to herding them by making half circles wide enough that they took his notion and trotted eastward. There were eleven in the bunch, and he'd let Landers cull one of

75

them or buy all of them. The steers were calico in color, with bands of yellow, black, and mahogany across their bodies. All of them must have shared a common ancestry with some old bull and his kin in the thick live oak beyond the Llano. Their long black and white horns shone in the high morning sun as they took a single-file line of march.

They were a fat enough lot, and their hair glistened. Maybe he wasn't asking the army enough. Fifty a head sounded like a high price to him, but Crawford might bellyache about it. He sent Rough charging to the right, and his movement reset the line of the steers' course more eastward across the rolling plains.

At mid-afternoon, they bailed off the tall bank for a drink from the shimmering Powder. He could see the activity in the camp across the stream as he rode wide of the cattle and went to find Captain Landers. The Sioux women and children were mostly in the center of the camp, with small tents and canvas shades set up.

He was anxious to see about Doe's welfare too, but he'd have to conceal his interest. As he forded the river, he recalled Murdock's grim killing of another scout, Charlie Dog, a Delaware. They'd been chasing down rumors of Cheyennes in Kansas. Slocum had lost a good horse of his own during their five-day search for hostiles, and was riding a half-broke mule back to camp along with four other scouts including Murdock, Charlie Dog, a Ponca called Hicks, and Joe Claymore, an ex-Confederate soldier.

"Charlie Dog, I want to buy that whore that shares your blankets," Murdock announced.

Riding beside him, Charlie frowned at Slocum as if he did not believe the man's words. Then he shrugged and kept riding his long-necked roan.

"You can't do her any good with your short dick," Murdock announced, causing everyone to look hard at him. Was he crazy?

"Ignore him, he's in a mean mood," Hicks warned Charlie as he pushed his horse in close.

"He better close his filthy mouth about my squaw," Charlie said under his breath.

"Dammit, you heard me, you surly red dog."

"Cut it out," Slocum said. "You don't need to pick on him."

"I pick on who I want to. Shut up, you rebel bastard, or I'll have you brought up on charges," the big man said.

"Watch your tongue, Murdock," Claymore said.

"Same goes for you, Claymore."

"You taking on all of us?" Claymore asked with his hand on his gun butt.

His face a mask of heated rage, Murdock spurred his horse and galloped ahead of them.

"He's not getting my woman," Charlie said, and his black eyes drilled holes in the retreating back of the buckskinner.

"Don't let him anger you," Hicks said. "That's what he wants."

"I will kill him if he ever calls her such a name again."

"Can't you see he wants you mad?" the Ponca asked with concern.

Slocum had enough trouble with handling the mule, but his gut feeling was there would be more and deeper trouble before the sun set. Murdock had started the conflict on purpose, and would never be satisfied until he had his way. As Slocum used both hands to jerk the bits and keep the wall-eyed jackass in control, he wondered when the big man would make his move.

Charlie's new wife Blue Bird was a nice-looking girl in her finery. The beaded deerskin wedding dress had cost many dollars, and she wore it about the scout camp proudly. Her beauty had caught many male eyes since he brought her from the Indian lands in the south. Everyone had congratulated the Delaware on his shrewd choice. In addition to her beauty, she was never lazy and worked hard to clean his clothes and fix his meals. Her tepee area was swept each day, and she threw rocks at dogs that threatened to defecate in her "yard."

The small river ahead was in a deep cut, and the banks were crowded with willows. Forced to dismount, they had to lead their mounts down to water them. Slocum tried to loosen the girth, but his mule shied and he found himself on the end of the reins being half-dragged around by the animal.

"You need help?" Charlie asked, riding in close.

"No," Slocum said, and worked up the leather leads with the intention of either subduing the mule or killing him.

Laughing at his plight, the Delaware dismounted. Then he went up the steep bank leading his pony and left Slocum to his own devices. The last sight he had of the scout's unblocked black hat with the eagle feather in the band was when Slocum reached the stubborn critter and tried to kick in his belly with his boot toe. Mule and man went round and round, tearing up grass.

The black mule finally surrendered and dropped his head. Then two shots were fired down by the river and, as if under fire, the mule plunged off, dragging Slocum face-down through the brush and thistles on the end of the lines. The head stall finally broke, and the mule left for another land popping stirrups as he bucked away through the trees.

"He's killed Charlie!" Hicks shouted as he came into view out of breath.

"Dammit!" Slocum swore, undecided about what to do next. His saddle rifle and personal items were strapped on the missing mule, and obviously Hicks wanted his help with Charlie.

"I'm coming," Slocum said. That damn Murdock wasn't getting by with this.

They meet Claymore by the body. Obviously Charlie had been in the water, for his leather shirt was soaked, and the blood on his chest told the story as Slocum dropped to his knee. Charlie's eyes closed when Slocum knelt beside him; the Delaware had obviously gone to see his Maker and there was nothing they could do.

"Shot him in the back," Claymore said, and shook his head.

"You seen him do it?" Slocum asked, looking around at the tall cut banks that walled in the river.

"No."

"You seen Murdock?" Slocum asked Hicks.

The Indian shook his head warily.

"We all were separated coming off that bank and busy watering our horses," Claymore said. "Next thing, I heard the shots and ran up here. Charlie was pitched in the water, shot in the back."

"It's going to be damn hard to prove to an army court he did it." Slocum listened to a blue jay scolding them as the futility of their proving anything against Charlie's killer made a large empty pit in his stomach.

"Gawdamn backshooter," Claymore said through his teeth. "We all heard him threaten Charlie back there."

"I know, but proving it is another thing."

"What we do?" Hicks asked.

"Bury him." Slocum exhaled as he wearily rose to his feet. He owed Murdock for killing the Delaware. There was no sign of anyone up in the walnuts and cottonwoods high above them. They might be lucky themselves to survive the ride back to Camp Day. He still had to find his wild mule or walk back the last fifty miles.

Now, as he crossed the Powder, the knee-deep water swept past Rough's legs. Up the other bank, he searched for the officers' row of tents and Captain Landers. Under the snapping flag, a sentry stopped him.

"I'm here to see the captain."

"Yes sir, I will tell him—"

"Not necessary, Private." The short officer emerged from the flap, returned the private's salute, and then put on his Stetson campaign hat. "I figured it was you, Slocum. Did you locate the cattle I requested?"

"They're across the river and I brought eleven. I must say they are spooky range cattle and it will require several riders to surround and corral them," Slocum added as he dismounted, then extended his hand to the man. They shook warmly.

"How did you get them here by yourself?" A frown formed on his frosted brows as the officer looked at him.

"Mostly luck." Slocum smiled.

"I doubt that. Sergeant O'Reilly, have a troop mount up. We are going to corral those cattle that are across the river."

"Sir, if I might?" Slocum asked.

"Go ahead."

"Sergeant, I'd circle them wide and not whoop a lot or they'll go back to Texas."

"Ayee, sir, we shall," the big noncom said, and turned to his men.

"You don't need to buy the eleventh one," Slocum offered.

"No problem. We will need it. I sent a dispatch for the command to send several wagons to transport the women and children to Standing Rock. That might require an act of Congress, since the army has such limited funds these days. But I assure you I have complete authority to write you a warrant for the beef."

"Those women and children are in poor condition to walk there."

"Exactly, and they aren't warriors, just women and children caught in the middle."

"I wondered about them when I saw them."

"Yes. They were half-starved, and that's why we need to wait for transportation and clothing for them. I know if some large Eastern newspapers ever got hold of another Trail of Tears story, why, it could change an election."

Slocum agreed.

"Let's go get some coffee at the mess tent. O'Reilly will have those cattle in the pen and we can close your business. How many men are with you?"

"Right now me. Crawford is bringing up a crew from Texas this fall to round them up and ship them."

"Big country for one man to look after."

Slocum agreed as they took seats across from each other at the table under the canvas fly. He could see the squaws wearing discarded army shirts and blankets as they went about tending fires and carrying water. Naked children raced about shouting and laughing as if they were at ease among the blue coats. He saw some of the spirit had returned to them. Where was Doe?

He'd seen a few breed scouts talking, but no sign of Murdock, he realized as the captain spoke quietly to a corporal who'd approached the table.

"It seems my main scout has an errant wife again," Landers said, turning back as the corporal left and a private brought them steaming coffee in china cups.

"Murdock?"

"Yes. His wife left him sometime in the night and he has left too—I guess to go find her. She must not like his bed. According to him, she ran off with a Frenchman before and he found her in the Sioux camp. Obviously she was the one who stole your bay horse. She was well dressed and in good condition compared to the others when we found their camp."

"Yes, I saw her yesterday."

"A striking-looking woman for an Indian." Landers stirred sugar in his coffee. Then an aide came with a message and the officer excused himself.

Slocum looked out at the milling captives. Which way had Doe and Murdock gone? The tiny handle of the porcelain cup felt strange on his fingers as he considered the brown liquid. How long since he had drunk from a porcelain cup? A long time. Perhaps not since before the war, at home in Georgia. Damn, even now he could hear someone playing the grand piano and the swish of petticoats and expensive silk dresses. Even smell the lavender scent of perfume when Penelope Hayes bent over and in a whisper asked him if he would meet her on the veranda. His face was almost flushed as he looked down at the rounded cups and her cleavage. Then, as she straightened, she smiled openly at him from behind her Chinese fan, and he knew exactly what she wanted him to do.

Under the spreading magnolias, they rushed from the porch to the stables, where they entered the tack room and paused among the harness, saddles, and leather goods smelling of oil. Out of breath, she began to hoist up her many layers of clothes as the starlight flooded in the window above them.

"I daresay, John dear, we must hurry. I hope I am not a mess when you finish," she said, bending over, still fussing to raise the clothes and expose her shapely bare behind.

"I will be careful," he said, fumbling with weak fingers at the buttons to his fly. Before him, the bare half-moons of her bottom shone in the pearly light as she lay belly-down across the saddle stand.

Stiffly he scooted his feet to stand close behind her, his heart pounding like a runaway deer. With his pants down to his knees, the fear of their being discovered hung like a sharp-edged sword ready to plunge into his bare backside as he worked furiously to stiffen his root.

"You hard enough yet?" she whispered impatiently.

What if she changed her mind? What would he do then? His weak hand slid across the forbidden skin of her shapely behind, and he felt faint at the mere touch. The night sounds of the loft boards creaking under the weight of the sweet hay caught his breath.

"Try to put it in," she pleaded.

"I will."

"Oh, John darling, I have dreamed all week long about this—"

So had he. Shaken, he moved against her, the sensation of her cool skin against his drawing more of his strength. He paused with his manhood in his fist under her. Would he be big enough? Long enough? Would he satisfy her?

"Not in there! More up front. Oh, yes, in there!" she cried.

When he entered her slippery gates, he knew. The fear

of discovery evaporated and a new-felt eagerness to consume her took over. He clutched her bony hip bones and tried to go deeper and deeper, pounding against her hard butt as she groaned and cried for more. He was giving her all he had. Was it enough? He knew some men were hung like stallions.

Then he knew that he was about to erupt, and desperately he clutched himself hard to her, in as deep as he could strain to go. Finally drained, he came out, stumbling back until he found a barn post to support himself as he watched her adjust her clothes in the slits of starlight that came through the barn's wall. She was busy putting her petticoats down with some effort, and her hair looked a little tousled, but she looked beautiful to him.

"Well, darling, you are sure learning since the first time," she said, and ran her index finger under his chin. "I must get back. That Randy Swaid wants a dance. But darling, I swear that he ain't got half as much root as you have. Not even half as big around as yours is either. Bye now." She stood on her toes and kissed him.

Half as much, huh?

"I think they are going to get those cattle in the corral," Captain Landers said, standing beside the tent post with his cup in hand.

"Yes," Slocum said, returning to the moment, and rose to join the man with the coffee in his hand as twenty troopers on horseback and several more on foot with blankets crowded the cattle into the pole pens. When the troopers were finished, Landers set the cup down and they both strode down the camp to examine his herd.

"Good job, men." Landers said, and climbed the fence. The longhorns milled some and sniffed the hay suspiciously. Landers counted them and then studied them carefully.

"They are fat and in good condition. I was raised on a farm in Vermont and know animal condition. Those animals should be eatable," the officer said, climbing down. "I'll take all eleven. Come on up and we shall fill out the warrant for them."

"You mind if I talk to a few of the Sioux women?" Slocum asked.

"No." The man frowned with a question on his face.

"I lost a locket this summer. Thought maybe if they had it or had found it, they might sell it back."

"Gold one?"

"Yes, sir, a family one."

"Go ahead. I'll fix up the papers."

Slocum figured one lie was as good as another. He spotted the tall woman who had headed the butchering. She wore a faded blue shirt and a skirt of blue cloth. Maybe she would know where Doe went. She blinked at his approach. He shook his head as she started to rise from the cooking fire.

He squatted down and looked around to be certain their words would be private from the soldiers in the area. None seemed interested in his speaking to her, so he turned back and faced her.

"You speak English?" he asked.

"Some," she said.

"Doe has left. Did she go to join her brother?"

"Long Knife?"

"Yes."

The woman looked around, and then she nodded.

"Can she get to him before Murdock catches her?"

She shrugged her thin shoulders without an answer, and then reached over to stir the stew in the pot. The smell of the cooking meat made him hungry. He nodded and patted her on the shoulder.

"This blue legs chief is a good man," he said. "Listen to him. He sends for wagons to take you to Standing Rock."

She acknowledged his words. "Maybe some day you can kill Murdock."

"He needs it," he said, and straightened.

Considering his new information, he crossed the parade ground and the sentry showed him inside the captain's quarters. The flag flapped on the staff above and the sides of the tent popped in the wind as the sun filtered through the canvas in a warmth that was almost stifling.

Landers handed him the paper. He read the amount and signature. Then he placed the warrant inside his shirt and shook hands with the man. *Old man, I've sold eleven more head. Now I must go find her.*

13

The Bighorns loomed before him. Snowcapped, the highest steel-gray peaks rose like great points against skyline. He'd found enough tracks of a shod horse to know he was back on Murdock's trail. There was no time to drop by the cow camp for supplies, so he'd detoured by the store to buy some jerky, hardtack, and cheese. Grateful that the Jacksons weren't around, he'd paid Thurman, taken his purchases, and ridden back to Murdock's tracks, which led westward up into a deep canyon's yawning mouth. By then sundown had closed in at the base of the range, and rather than ride into a blind alley or an ambush, he camped for the night beside a small stream.

The flash of hungry trout feeding on surface insects caught his eye, and he soon had his sleeve rolled up and was lying belly-down with his right arm immersed in the water. After a miss or two, with his hand almost cramped from the icy water, he finally grasped a fat fish and quickly tossed its slick form up on the bank. Then, on his feet, flexing his cold arm to restore circulation, he went to the flopping silver creature. From his boot sheath, he drew out his long knife. The fish was swiftly gutted and the blood washed out of its backbone in the twilight where Slocum squatted on the stream edge. He cooked his catch on green limbs over a small fire as the night crept like a black bear over the mountains and the stars came out.

Seated on the ground in the campfire's light, he ate the rich pink flesh with his fingers and enjoyed the luxury of the meat. He studied the fire's blue-red flames and wondered how far he had to go to find her. Murdock would be a formidable enemy when they met, but he held no personal dread of the man. His only concern was what Murdock might do to her in his anger. The flakes of fish on Slocum's tongue began to lose their flavor as he thought about the scout catching up with her and venting his fury on her.

Then, as the night's cold settled in the canyon, he began to realize where the lash marks on her back had come from. She had disobeyed Murdock before. This time the madman might beat her to death if Slocum didn't find her in time. He listened to night owl's hoot and the snort of Rough standing hip-shot and asleep in the darkness under the pine trees boughs. *I'm coming, Doe, with the morning light.*

At sunup, he had no time for foolishness from the horse as they started up the canyon, and he quickly checked any plans Rough had to pitch. Obviously the hard riding and lack of enough feed had tempered the bay, and he struck out the steep canyon pathway like a broken horse. Ahead over the great divide, Slocum knew, was a place the Indians called Ten Sleep. That meant it required ten days or nights to get there from Fort Laramie on the way to Yellowstone, or ten days or nights to come from Yellowstone back to there.

As he climbed the V-shaped canyon's steep pathway, he could look back across the blue plains that stretched back hundreds of miles to the Black Hills, the Powder River basin, and the place at the base of these mountains where Indians a decade before had slaughtered Fetterman and his company. Bloody grounds. He could recall the large herds of buffalo that roamed the land when he freighted up to the Montana gold fields on the Bozeman Trail from Fort Laramie. The shaggy beasts were all gone, save for perhaps a few left in Montana and maybe Yellowstone. Soon no one would recall what the boss of the prairie even looked like.

Grateful for the warming sun on his back, he rode up the canyon using the well-worn path. Gray rock covered the steep ground with a short grass carpet on the sides that rose above him. Patches of aspen dotted the side canyons that fed into the main one that he and Rough climbed. It was a vulnerable place to be, but the ways to enter the Bighorns were few and he felt this one was a main route. An occasional sight of the familiar shoe prints in the dust told him enough to keep urging the bay horse on.

The clack of Rough's iron shoes on the rocks rang like a bell, and echoed and re-echoed as the seam in the mountain grew narrower near the top. The bay cat-hopped the last hundred yards, and then huffed for his breath in the thin air as Slocum reined up and surveyed the vast grassland that opened before him. Four large racked bucks raised their heads and then trotted away.

Ordinarily he would have downed one for meat, but there was no time for that. He paused to admire their wide antlers as they stopped to consider him. They tossed their horns in threat, then reconsidered and moved up into the timber.

He drew a deep breath of the rarified air tinged with pine, and then he booted Rough on his way. The long open meadow twisted and rolled westward bordered by thick forests. He followed the tracks. Maybe she had escaped Murdock. Slocum could hope a lot of things, but Murdock was a hound on a trail. Grimly Slocum remembered him from their Kansas scouting. The big man could part thick tall bluestem and see the minutest detail. Murdock knew how to track down whoever he wanted.

A shudder of cold ran up Slocum's spine and made him shiver under his shirt, and he dug out his jumper from the bedroll as he rode west. It was a lot cooler up here than down on the Powder. A sharp wind swept the grass, and he watched three antelopes stop on a high place to observe his passing. He smiled at them. A ways further on, he caught sight of a sow bear herding her cubs from a small marshy lake in a side canyon a hundred yards below the ridge he rode across.

He reined in the bay to let him breathe again. Clouds were piling up in the north. There would be an afternoon shower somewhere up here. For a long moment he watched the mother bruin drive her babies until they disappeared in the security of the woods. He twisted around trying to study the high points to mark his way back. Then satisfied that he could move on, he jabbed the horse with his heels. Here the sign of hoofprints in the dry gray dirt was hazy, and he was using his intuition more than scouting skills to continue westward.

Trees grew shorter and the trail entered a dense growth of lodgepoles. A narrow alleyway wound skyward through the downed timber, which was so thick he doubted that a man could ever cross it on foot if he stepped off the well-worn pathway. Higher and higher they went, the air cooler and harder to breath, so by noon he had a high-country headache pounding at his temples. Rough began to show the fatigue, and Slocum had to dismount, walk, and lead the horse to save him.

Then he reached a high open saddle pass and the trail split. One way went north, and the other led down into an endless grassy alpine meadow toward the west. He let Rough graze while he studied the faint tracks. He chewed on jerky from his saddlebags as he walked out in the short brown grass in a great circle looking for a sign or print he might recognize. If he took the wrong fork here it might cost Yellow Doe her life.

He watched two sassy magpies in their black-white

plumage come sailing in to investigate his business there
and then to pick at the horse's steaming apples for any
feed in the droppings. They soon tired of that, and flew
away to the west. Undecided, Slocum pushed his hat
back and scratched his forehead. Which way should he
choose?

West was his choice of direction, like the magpies.
Maybe they had told him something. He caught the bay
and mounted up. They rode down the wide valley watered by a small clear stream and followed it north, still
not seeing much sign.

Several miles down the grassy meadow, he looked
over an incoming trail that went up a side canyon. No
horse had recently been ridden up the dirt path cut in
the sod. Still, it was more than a game trail, so he rose
in the stirrups to stretch his tired back, using his saddlehorn for balance. He tried to see some sign of life up
the grassy swale hemmed in by the slopes covered with
thick timber.

On a chance he reined Rough up the side trail, and
soon the sod-covered roof of a small log cabin came
into view. He felt for his .44 and then, after looking all
around at the timbered walls that hemmed him in, he
pushed the horse on. It was the first sign of civilization
since he had left the store, and probably belonged to
some miner, or had been abandoned by some settler who
had come up in the summer hoping to claim a home-
stead, not realizing the violence of the winter that struck
hard in this range.

He dismounted and eased himself out of the saddle
close to the cabin. Six-gun in his hand, he looked around
at the sound of a gurgling spring that rushed out of a
steep hillside a hundred yards above him. The place
looked like heaven—if there wasn't a rattlesnake in the
cabin, or Murdock.

He stepped up on the logs that served as the porch
and reached for the door latch with his left hand. Hammer cocked back, he was ready.

''Slocum!'' the voice shouted behind him.

14

His heart stopped as he turned at the familiar voice. Doe dropped the three large trout on the limb stringer that she carried and rushed down the steep slope. He tried twice to holster his Colt, and almost forgot to disarm it in his excitement. Finally he stopped and, holding the .44 with the muzzle up, spun the cylinder to the empty, released the hammer, and jammed it in as she reached him in her headlong flight.

Her force sent him on his butt, and they began to laugh as she climbed up his frame and began to hold his face in her long fingers and kiss him. Flat on his back, he looked into her brown eyes and could hardly believe his good fortune.

"Murdock is up here somewhere," he said. "And I may have led him to you."

"I don't care, you are safe." She tossed her braids aside, pressing him to the ground. "I was worried that you would kill him at the army camp and they would hang you for it."

"I was worried he might have found you up here."

"You should not have come here." She dropped her head and looked at him with disapproval.

"Why? Are your brother and the others near here?" He tried to look around, but she still held him down with her hands pressing down his shoulders.

"No, they have gone to the land of steam shoots and hot springs. Yellowstone."

"Why there?" He frowned at their decision to leave the sanctuary of the Bighorns and cross the vast open country between the two ranges.

"They hope to find the spirit again."

"Why didn't you go with them?"

"They did not want a woman to go." He saw the sadness gathering behind her brown eyes.

"I am sorry," he said to comfort her.

"When men have lost all hope, they do not think wisely." Then she rose up and helped him to his feet. "I will remove the prints of your horse and then we will hide him with mine."

"I'll go with you."

"No, you will leave more prints." She shook her head while picking up a broom of pine boughs from near the wall. "I will not be long. Put the saddle in the cabin and I will return."

He unsaddled the bay and then took the rig inside. The small room was low, but the homeyness of the crude table and chairs cheered him. Beyond, her fancy blankets were spread over a pine-branch bed that looked inviting to him. He felt his beard stubble, and went to the small sheet-iron stove that someone with much effort had packed in there. Checking on the water in the kettle, he found it hot enough to use for his needs. He took out his small mirror and shaving things. The light through the translucent deer hide stretched over the south window would be enough to see by. He began lathering his face, and soon was busy slicing away the whiskers. He looked up as she rushed in out of breath.

He paused in his stroke. "Everything fine?"

"No sign." She wrinkled her nose to dismiss any concern. ''I will take your horse up in the high country put him with mine.''

''Wait—''

''You shave whiskers! I be back quick.'' Her wink was enough to warm him.

''Sure thing,'' he agreed, and waved her out.

He had finished his shave and was standing in the doorway waiting for her as she came back, fringe flying and the braids trailing in her haste.

''Whose place is this?'' he asked as she snuggled in his arms.

''I don't know, but for many years this cabin has been here,'' she said, hugging him tight and burying her face in his chest.

''I was here once in this valley with Sitting Bull,'' she went on. ''The cabin was here then and the men argued much about burning it, but since there was no one living here, some of the wise men of the tribe said it would be good to stay in if we had to come up here in winter. Later that summer somewhere west of here in the mountains, I remember that we fought the blue legs and then we split up and met again on the Tongue.''

''How did you escape Murdock?'' he asked, hugging her head to him.

''I feared you would come for me.'' She nestled her face on his chest. ''I knew I could not go to your camp. He would come there and kill you.''

''I do not fear Murdock.''

''No! But my spirits have warned me about you and him.'' She closed her eyes and shook her head. ''It will not be a good thing. I fear for your life. It is why I went away. I thought you would never find me here.''

''Two magpies showed me the way.''

She snickered as he squeezed her. Then their mouths found each other and the fire rose inside him. Clothes flew away in all directions, he toed his boots off, and soon both were stripped to their skin. The cool cabin air soon rushed over their naked bodies as they hurried to jump in the bed.

The fury consumed them as he knelt between her spread legs and cupped her firm breasts in his hands. How could he have ever let her stay one moment in the company of Murdock? Never again would he lose her. He promised himself that never again would he let her go as he drew in the heady, hot air of the fire that their passion kindled.

Impatient for him to begin, she reached for his stem, plunged his rock-hard knob inside her, and then scooted under him. Her long slender arms drew him downward, and their mouths sealed the bargain as his hips moved to seek her.

Pine boughs bent under their furious passion. His body jackknifed again and again to meet her arched back. Both sought to be welded together. He strove to penetrate her as deeply as a well, and she tried to accommodate his efforts. Swept away in the whirlpool of their fury, her mouth half open, she moaned pleasure's cry and tossed her head from side to side. Then her fingernails raked the skin on his back like a cougar's claws. Finally, driven in desperation for some relief from their wildfire flames of pleasure, she grasped the cheeks of his butt in her hands to pull him deeper inside her, and sunk her nails like stilettos deep into his flesh. Caught up in her own release, she cried out in a shrill voice with her legs stretched skyward and flailing the air in wild abandon. Then, like a flame blown out, she collapsed in a faint under him. Her lids were half closed under the thick lashes, and she mumbled his name in her drugged state as he raised up to study her and sought to regain some air in his aching lungs.

With a grin at her helplessness, he gave her a small shove on the hip and rolled her over onto her knees. She gave a small groan of protest as she rose to her hands and knees on top of the springy bed. On his own knees, he moved up to her bottom, which shone like lustrous copper in the diffused light from the deerskin window.

"Are you ready for more?" he asked in her ear.

"Yes," came her husky answer.

With care he reached under and re-inserted himself in her slick gates. She tossed her braids as if to clear her head as she raised it to prepare for more. Then he bent over, grasped her breasts in each hand, and began to seek her again.

His actions soon rekindled the fires in her, and she began to push hard at his intrusion. Inside, her muscles began to contract like a vise. Her head was thrown back, the cries of her needs grew loud, and his driving became faster and harder, until at last he exploded inside her in a final burst that drove him tight against her butt. He half-lifted her off the bed, squeezing her tight around her middle to savor the final depleting moment of their glory. Then they crashed into a pile, and in his groggy state he managed to pull a cover over them.

15

Where was Murdock? Slocum sat on his haunches and studied the edge of the dark timber. He had been on his guard for three days. They'd even killed a fat elk yearling in the high country above the cabin, and had returned expecting to find the scout waiting at the cabin, but there was still no sign of him. Slocum drew out a cigar and lighted it as he tried to imagine what had happened to the man.

Deep in thought, he drew in the smoke and then exhaled. Murdock was up to some kind of no good. In the morning, Slocum planned to leave her and go check on the cattle. They could have drifted to Montana by this time. But he didn't wanted to leave her without settling with the scout first. He half-shrugged. There was no way to end anything with Murdock—he would have to kill him, period. Sooner or later, for her safety, he would have to do it. The sweet smoke of the cigar settled some of his anxiousness, and he rose to his feet and went to the gurgling spring for a drink.

''You can come here again,'' she said from where she

fleshed the green elk hide on the turned-up log end. The pinkish side stretched tight as she applied the small razor-sharp knife to the small remains of muscles and meat attached to it. He nodded that he had heard her, and then used the gourd dipper to take a drink of water.

"The only thing," he said with a deep sigh, wiping his wet mouth on his kerchief, "I have five hundred steers down there to worry about. You should come back to the cow camp."

"No, I would never feel safe there with the blue legs camped so close. They know who I am and they would return me to him for he has told them I am his wife."

"Tell them that you divorced him."

She shook her head no. "I am safer here."

"You damn sure *aren't* safer here. I don't know where he is right now, but he may be in that timber right up there." He scanned the sage and grass meadow that floored the valley for any signs.

"You are angry that you came here?" she asked, making herself busy with her hide, jerking it up in a new position.

"No. I am angry that Murdock hasn't shown his worthless hide up here."

"I am glad you came, and the elk meat will do me many moons."

"In the fall . . . I mean when this cattle business is over . . ." He wished he could find the words to make a commitment. "If I come up here, can we spend the winter in that cabin?"

"You know I would be very happy."

"Well, don't hold out for it to happen, because lots can happen between now and then. I don't always get to do what I want to do."

"I will understand," she said, busying herself with the skin.

"No, you don't. But it's too complicated for me to explain it all."

He drew the cigar down and ground the butt out under his heel. No one could count on him. He might have to ride off without a word. There were men on his back trail and they never gave up. Bounty men that never slept. He closed his eyes at the notion of being on the run again.

She rose, set the knife down, and soon stood before him. Her long fingers, strong with the copper smell of the elk skin, pulled his face to hers with an immediacy. Soon the sweetness of her mouth spilled into his own. Her tenderness drove the blinding anger of his situation away the way a gust of prairie wind made a puff of smoke vanish.

"If you must ride, I would go with you." Her deep pools of brown were pleading with him.

"Then come to the cow camp. I can guard you there."

"No, this is my place. I would never sleep there."

"I must return in the morning." He drew a deep breath and narrowed his eyes as he studied the distant range to the west. "I've been gone too long now."

"I will be here when you return." She smiled for him.

He swept her up into his arms and then lifted her up to hold her higher. Looking taken aback, she began to laugh out loud at his action and put her arms around his neck.

"I will never get that hide tanned at this rate." She shook her head in disapproval close to his.

"After today you will have plenty of time by yourself to tan hides," he said as he turned sideways to pass through the door into the cabin with her in his arms. In long strides he crossed the room, and then unceremoniously dumped her on the bed.

"I suppose you want me undressed?" she asked, sitting up and trying to look put out at him.

"Either way," he said with a wink, and toed off his boots.

In the cool gray light of dawn, huddled in his jumper for warmth, he mounted his cow pony. Twice, Rough tried his best to throw him. But Slocum finally let him buck his heart out across the high meadow where Doe had kept the gelding with her horse. Then Slocum waved at her as she stood holding her own pony far back down the clearing. He set Rough into a trot on his course, a long circle to the north away from the cabin.

She had shown him a way out on the elk hunt, how to slip past a small silver lake and then work his way back west so he rode past the end of her valley and out to the magpies' pass.

The sun was up in the sky when he rode over the high saddle and started down through the narrow pathway that bisected the fallen tangled lodgepole timber. He rounded a turn, and a large male bear rose in their path. Rough had enough and snorted as if he'd seen the devil, then piled sideways into a tree smashing Slocum's leg.

The bear's roar was loud enough in his ears for the section hands to hear it in Cheyenne as Slocum fought for the Winchester. The shot of pain in his leg from the collision with the tree proved distracting enough that he was slow drawing the long gun.

His first shot from atop the spooked horse went wild. He levered another cartridge in as Rough crawfished uphill seeking an opening in the timber to escape the raging bruin. Slocum's second bullet struck the bear in the shoulder and he screamed in pain, swatting his claws within inches of the crazed horse.

The next shot would be Slocum's last as the bear charged in rage. He dared to stand in the stirrups, aiming off the backing horse into the savage face of the crazed animal. His bullet slammed into the bear's brain. Then Slocum was forced to drop the rifle as he regained his balance on the deranged cow pony and fought Rough to a standstill, sawing with both hands on the bits.

He dismounted from the trembling horse, and his right leg proved barely able to hold his weight. Something serious was wrong with it. Hopping around, he examined the damage done to his mount's shoulders and neck. The claw marks on Rough were only superficial, he decided, holding the reins wrapped around his hand as the wide-eyed cow pony snorted in sheer fear and tried to flee him and the dead bear.

"Easy, he's dead or near dead." Slocum drew his Colt and shot the bear in the skull again to be certain. He held tight to the reins with his left hand as his horse shook his head and half-reared to escape the shooting and the deceased bruin. Panicked by the unmoving pile in the middle of the narrow corridor through the lodgepoles, Rough dragged Slocum back up the trail despite his efforts to sooth the cow pony.

Dead bear or not, they had to go by it to get off the mountain. Slocum's sore right leg had begun to swell, and soon he might be unable to even ride. He hated to simply waste the bear, but under the circumstances he needed to get on. The pile of shit-stinking black hair was an obstacle he needed to get his horse past, but he wondered how he would ever do it as he fought to hold the terror-driven animal.

"Dammit, Rough, there ain't a way for miles around this thicket and that dead bear. We've got to get off this mountain today and soon," Slocum said as they moved backwards up the steep trail. His patience on a short fuse, forgetting his weakened right leg, he tried to kick the horse in the belly to get his attention. His efforts ended when the horse jerked him off his feet. He was dragged along on the rocky pathway on his knees, and was forced to grasp the reins in both hands until Rough finally backed into some trees. Then, goosed forward by their branches, the anxious cow pony must have mistaken them for more bears for he almost jumped astraddle Slocum, who was scrambling to his feet.

The opportunity to mount came when the horse stopped beside him. Slocum swung in the saddle and screamed at the horse, lashing him with the rein ends. The startled cow horse bolted forward. Then seeing what lay in his path, Rough gathered up under saddle and rider and flew over the carcass in a leap that would have cleared Hell's Canyon. He lost his footing landing on the other side, and only by scrambling in the loose rocks on the path did he ever stand up enough to finally regain his feet. The saddlehorn was gouging a new belly button in Slocum's stomach as he pushed himself up to a sitting position and reined the trembling horse to a halt.

Then he dismounted, weak from his efforts, and used his reata to tie Rough to a nearby sapling. Favoring his sore leg, he hobbled up the trail past the dead bear and retrieved his Winchester from the trail. The rifle looked okay as he brushed the dirt and rotten needles from it. With a long sigh, he started back for his horse. His lower right leg hurt worse with each passing minute, and the trip back required him to stop several times, set down the long gun, use a tree for support as he flexed his knee back and forth to try to drive out some of the pain out of the calf, then pick up the gun and limp ahead some more.

Before he remounted, he sat down on a large boulder and removed his boot; his foot had swollen, and in another half hour he'd have never gotten the boot off short of cutting it to pieces. Hopping around after the uneasy horse, he finally managed to tie the boot to his saddle horn. With the rifle back in the saddle boot, he undid the lead rope, talking gently to the white-eyed pony, and then gathered the reins, giving a last look back at the black humped rug lying thirty yards up the trail, and swung up on Rough.

The cow pony left out at a trot almost too fast for the downhill grade of the trail. The stench of the bear was still in Slocum's nose as he leaned over, rubbed his sore right leg, and ducked the low limbs. He didn't need any more troubles for one day.

16

He fell out of the saddle in the darkness. The pain shot up his right hip like a grave-digger bolt of lightning. His fingers fumbled to undo his bedroll as he tried to stand on one foot. The rain had quit. It had plagued him all afternoon, and he could still see some blue flashes to the north as the rain moved away from his cow camp.

His sock was wet where he'd touched his toe in the mud; his right leg was swollen as big as his head. In a last effort, he threw the bedroll down and then led Rough to the corral. He might need him saddled if his leg got worse.

"Sorry, old boy, I'll unsaddle you in the daylight," he promised, and then took the bridle off the weary, snorting Rough. Limping out unsteadily, he put up the poles, pausing to let the bolts of heated lightning die down in his right side. When the pain partially subsided, he hobbled, using only the right toe to balance himself, and finally got to his bedroll. He dragged it to the tent. Tossing it inside the front flap, he dropped to the ground and then crawled inside dragging himself much like the crippled Sioux woman he'd seen in the canyon. He was in a hell of a mess, and he needed to figure a way out fast.

He awoke in a cold sweat and heard men talking in the darkness. There was something familiar in their words. He felt for his Colt and then sat up in his blankets. Was he dreaming? He cocked the hammer back, and then he knew the voice. Deveau was out there ordering someone around. Slocum's dizzy head swarmed; his swollen leg felt filled with hot needles.

"Take some of this, you sum-bitch!" And the blaze of the rustler's gun flashed outside, his bullets cutting holes in the tent as Slocum flattened himself on the ground hoping Deveau's aim was high.

"Let's get out the hell out of here!" someone else pleaded.

"This dumb horse is run in the ground," a third voice complained.

"Leave him then! *Sacre bleu* my gun is empty!" the Frenchman shouted as his hammer fell on empty chambers.

Slocum crawled to the flap and belly down, emptied his Colt after the men as they raced off into the night. Convinced he had only hastened their escape, he cursed as the bitter gun smoke made his eyes water. How in hell did they get out of jail?

He managed to drag himself across the wet grass to the fire ring, and then, lying on his side, managed to toss some of the last of the cedar wood into the ring. But the damp sappy wood would not ignite from his matches as he lay on the wet ground and tried to start the fire. Finally he got a flame started and used splinters for tinder, and soon a fire lighted the area. He sat up pleased with his effort.

Rough snorted in the night, and Slocum grinned. He might be hurt, but neither he nor the bay horse was dead. Damn you, Deveau, you should have ridden on to Canada when you busted out of that jail, instead of stopping here.

He dragged himself on his good knee to the chuck wagon. Pulling himself up, he wondered where the crutches were in the wagon. He recalled that one of Crawford's crew had hurt his leg when his horse had stepped in a prairie-dog hole. The cook, St. John, had found the man a pair of crutches in the supplies that they carried. The crutches should be in the wagon box somewhere. Slocum's problem was how to locate them while hopping around the damn outside and lifting the cover to feel for them. He groped inside, finding ropes and spare gear, but no crutches. They he moved painfully up on the sideboard, hoping St. John had left them in along the outside and not down under everything else.

Out of breath, he paused to recover. His fire cast an orange glow on the wagon's side. Deveau, Murdock— he had enough enemies in this land to last him a long time. Not to mention the Jackson twins. He had no time for this hurt leg. Then his fingers closed on the long sticks, and he dropped his forehead to the sideboard and let the sharpness in his right hip and limb ease before he brought the crutches out.

Mounted on the crutches, he moved quickly to find some grain for Rough. Then he needed to ride after Deveau. Obviously the three had taken Eagle, Brownie, and the packhorse. There was no sign of them on the flats around camp, and all the horses wouldn't have drifted that far away from camp. With his new aids to propel him, he carried the nose sack of corn to the saddled bay. Rough stood a good ways out from the open corral, but showed no signs of running off at his approach. Slocum hooked the muzzle on his face, then examined the dried blood in the claw marks on his chest and shoulder. *Too close for comfort, old boy.* He turned on his crutches and looked to the north. He needed a bait of food in his belly, and then he'd head out and find the Frenchman and his bucks. He owed them for what they did to his tent. The dollar-size holes burned into the canvas looked like Swiss cheese, and the tent would damn sure leak the next time it rained. With a wry grimace, he set out to fix some food. The bay was noisily chomping on the corn as Slocum swung himself across the ground back to the chuck wagon.

Those rustlers might have thought that Rough was jaded, but he was tough. He was Texas bred, and it was hard to kill such a wiry pony. Deveau had made a big mistake swinging by there. He would regret his second attack on the V Bar C outfit before many sunsets passed. Under the wagon flap, balanced on his sticks, Slocum ground some coffee beans. The stake ropes needed tightening, but they could wait.

Not escaping the swelling and aching in his leg, he managed to cook some fry bread and bacon. He drank enough coffee to finally make himself get up and empty his bladder. His eyes were on the far north horizon as he vented himself with the wind to his back, and he wondered how hard and fast the three rustlers would ride. Finished, he buttoned his fly with some effort with the crutches under his arm.

Later, with his bedroll, grain for his pony, some grub, and his crutches tied on Rough, he mounted and headed north. He only pushed the weary bay into a trot when the going was level and easy. The gait shook Slocum's swollen leg until the hurting blinded him. The rest of the time he let the cow pony pick his own way. It would be slow, but he'd find Deveau and the others. A sharp pain shot up his right side, then danced like lightning around his jawbone. He closed his eyes and arched his back with his teeth clenched until the bolts of hurting subsided.

Dizzy in the saddle, he grasped the horn to stay aboard; two horizons floated in the north as he fought the waves of dizziness. And this too would pass, he promised himself as he pushed on. The morning passed like a year, and several times he awoke, unsure that Rough had not turned back to camp during his own semi-consciousness. But a check of the sun to be sure of their direction, and then seeing the familiar horse prints in the dirt, made him feel satisfied each time, and he would boot the pony ahead.

By late afternoon, he had found a grassy bottom along a creek with some willows. It was as far as he could go. Like someone drunk, he unsaddled Rough, tied a leg rope on him, and then poured a bait of corn on a flat rock for the cow pony. With stiff fingers, he finally undid his bedroll, and then sat on it, drinking the last of his whiskey, which he had hoarded to cope with his pain. He sat on his blankets in a cold sweat and finished the fiery rye. Then he flung the bottle aside and bent over, intent on squeezing the hurting from his rock-hard leg and wishing for a moment's ease. He wasn't sure if the liquor helped, for he quickly lost consciousness and sprawled on his bedroll, feeling nothing.

"Slocum? Slocum?" It was Doe. He was dreaming, crazy, out of his head. The world blacked out again, and then he saw the low walled cabin in the sage and bunch grass. Was he back there? Making love to her subtle tawny body, her silky skin pressed to his him? Her rock-hard nipples pressed to the tangled black hair on his chest? Oh, hell, if there was a heaven, she had to be one of the angels there.

"What happened?" she asked as he looked at her.

He sat up. It was morning. He was still in his own camp.

"How long you been here?" he asked.

"Two days," she said, on her knees beside him.

"I've been out for two days?" He scratched his head in disbelief. "What are you doing here?"

"The army captured my brother on his way to Yellowstone. Two Moons escaped and came to tell me that they take him and the others to Standing Rock in wagons."

For the first time, Slocum saw the pie-faced buck squatted a few yards away.

"We tracked you here so I could tell you that I must go to Standing Rock and help Long Knife. He is very

angry and I can talk him out of doing anything crazy.''
Then she translated what she had spoken to Two Moons,
and he agreed with a nod.

''They stole my horses. Deveau and his bucks.''

''I saw the holes in the tent. I thought you were shot.''

''No, they couldn't hit a bull in the butt. I had every
intention of catching them and getting my horses back.''
He dropped his head and lifted his leg to move it.
''Guess I've lost the old man's ponies.''

She shook her head as if to dismiss his concern.

''Well, sitting here on my ass sure ain't going to get
them back.''

''I know where he will be,'' she said softly.

''Good,'' he said, reaching for her to help him get up.

''Rest one more day,'' she said, and pushed him
down.

''But—''

''Rest another day. My medicine is helping.''

''What medicine?''

''Willow bark boiled in water makes strong pain
killer. I have been feeding it to you.''

''I'll be damned,'' he said, and then smiled at her.
Even Two Moons smiled as the wind tousled the eagle
feathers in his braids.

If she knew Deveau's hideout, then maybe . . . He let
her push him back on his soagans. He was weaker than
he thought, and his head swarmed. He was back at the
cabin on the bed grasping her firm thighs to get closer.
His hips ached—*all dreams*.

17

After two days riding, they were in southern Montana. He figured they were in Crow country, somewhere near the Pryor Mountains. Two Moons led them along the edge of a mesa. He kept riding over to look off the edge and then back to them. Searching for a place for them to descend, is what Slocum figured he was up to. Rough had recovered and even tried to buck in the morning coolness, but Slocum had been ready and hauled his head up.

The willow tea had cut his aching to a serious stiffness. He wasn't sure if anything was broken, for his leg hung straight enough and his right foot looked the same as his left one. More sprained muscles than anything else, and there must have been lots of bleeding inside for his twice-larger leg had gone from purple to green.

"We close to them?" he asked her as they waited for Two Moons to return.

"Yes," she said above the wind that threatened to remove his hat. "They have a cabin and corral in a canyon along here. Two Moons will find it."

"You still going on to Standing Rock after this?"

"Yes. When you can ride." She wasn't looking at him.

"Will you be Two Moons's woman?" he asked, feeling an empty pit in his stomach over the loss.

"No. But I must help my people—"

"I know a place where we can hole up. Probably—"

"Slo-cum." She reached over and placed her long fingers on his forearm. "My people need me. Things will not be good on that reservation. They say that Sitting Bull does not like the queen's business. If he and the others come there, they too will need me. I speak good English and can reason with the angry ones."

Two Moons rode back to join them. He spoke sharply to her with a head toss to indicate that the rustlers were down below. Slocum nodded and rode as close as he dared. He dismounted, ground tied Rough and using one crutch, he hobbled close to the edge of the bluff. Then on his hands and knees, he crawled to the brink and laid down to study the small sod-roofed cabin. He removed his hat and the wind tossed his hair. A feeling of relief swept over him, for in his darkest hours, he had given up ever finding the old man's cowponies. He could see the gray in the corral with others that looked familiar to him at the distance.

"Should we wait until night?" he asked as Two Moons and Doe joined him, lying on their stomachs at the edge to peer at the camp.

She spoke to Two Moons.

He, in turn, shook his head.

Slocum rose to his knees and replaced his hat, *time to gather them up*.

They rode off the steep trail, out of the persistent wind at last. Two Moons, armed with his Winchester, led the way on his thin paint. Despite the pony's condition, he still went surefooted down the trail and carried his rider. A buffalo horse, no doubt—one of the last. Slocum turned to check on Doe as they rode under a great overhanging rock formation. Nothing that he said had changed her mind about staying up there while they took on the rustlers. He turned back at her nod that she was fine. Rough hesitated to pick his way around some slabs of talus rock and he booted him over it. *Hell, horse, it ain't a damn bear.*

"There!" Two Moons shouted as he pointed to someone coming out of the cabin. The figure saw them and ran back inside.

The war cry from the buck shattered the air. He urged the paint off the steep hillside in what Slocum considered the man's last suicide run. He unholstered his Colt with a serious head shake and then followed him, spurring Rough.

Puffs of gun smoke came from the doorway as Two Moons returned fire twice from horseback, guiding his pony northward across the face of the mountain. Slocum saved his shots and followed the man's course, wondering why he rode in that direction. Soon he could no longer see the front door of the cabin—only the back side—and realized that Two Moons sought to draw them outside.

The shooting from the cabin stopped and he saw that Doe was on their heels, pushing her pony in close. Two Moons dismounted among some house-sized rocks. Slocum, with a wary eye on the cabin, stepped down. She quickly gathered the reins from them and led the horses further away.

"What now?" he said to the buck as they both studied the rustler's hideout.

The buck made a sign and then snapped his fingers.

"Matches," Slocum said at his discovery. He felt in his vest and quickly produced a half dozen lucifers for the man.

Two Moons took them with a grin, then he ducked out and Slocum remained. Doe joined him. She climbed up higher for a better view of things.

"What's he going to do?" he asked.

She looked mildly in the direction that the buck had

gone, then turned back with a shrug. "Who knows, but he is a very good fighter."

"I see that."

"Does he know what Deveau did to you?"

"Yes," she said with a slow nod. "I told him about this man."

With her to watch, he decided to sit and wait. His leg was still stiff and throbbed from all the activity. Looked like they'd be there for a while. Those rustlers wouldn't be giving up easy. Maybe they'd have to starve them out. He feared it would be a long wait. How they'd ever—then she waved for him to join her.

He leaned over the rock and spotted Two Moons, a hundred yards downhill, dressed only in a loin cloth, wearing a porcupine quill vest. There was a band of red paint smeared across his nose and he was busy lighting fire arrows. He pointed the small bow high in the sky. In a great arch, trailing smoke, the missile thudded into the cabin's wall at the edge of the eaves and flames ran up to the overhanging roof boards. On the lee side, out of the wind, the fire soon began to consume the boards.

He checked his Colt and climbed over the rock. In a short while, they'd come out like flushed polecats. He hobbled down the hillside until he joined the grinning Two Moons.

"Good!" he said to the buck to congratulate him as the man traded the bow for the Winchester on the ground. Two Moons headed to where he could see the front door. Slocum worked his way after the nimble-footed brave. The obvious coughing and cursing of the inhabitants grew louder as they hurried to cover the front.

"Throw your guns out or we're cutting you down!" Slocum ordered from when he and Two Moons stood ready to cover their exit.

"Go to hell!" Deveau shouted and charged out, fighting the smoke with his left arm and shooting his six gun. Hatless, his black beard singed, he came charging out firing a hail of bullets that whizzed by Slocum's head.

The reply of their rifle and pistol shots doubled Deveau up and, hard hit, he soon sprawled on the ground. The other two outlaws came through the smoke-filled doorway with their hands held high, screaming that they gave up. In a tense moment watching their true intentions, Slocum held the smoking .44 in his fist—ready for anything. The two boys quickly cowered from the rifle-wielding Two Moons.

Doe rushed over to kneel by the dying Deveau, her knife poised. His eyes wide with fear, the dying outlaw tried to cower from the angry mask that glared down at him. Slocum holstered his pistol, then he stepped in and caught her hand.

"He's dying. It is enough," he said, pulling her to her feet.

"No, it is not! I wish to cut his manhood away while he still can feel it," she said, trying to break his vice-like grip on her forearms.

"He's going to die," he said.

"Yes, but he won't feel it then," she insisted, fighting his restrains with all her might. "I want him to cry in pain like he hurt me."

He swallowed hard and then he released her. It was not his way, but she was not his either. Without another word, he let her go past. Turning his back to her, he started for Two Moons and the boys. Deveau's shrill screams and pleading made shivers run up his spine, but he did not look back.

Sheer horror clouded the two youths' smoke-streaked faces as they watched her deliberate bloody mutilation of their leader. Two Moons nodded to Slocum and left the pair with him. The buck headed up the hill to retrieve his precious bow and other arrows, no doubt. The heat of the burning cabin on Slocum's back, at gun point he herded the two stunned rustlers after Two Moons.

He never looked back. Even when Doe rejoined them, he tried not to look at the smoke and flames of the cabin.

"I have brought your great gray horse," she said.

"Thanks," he said, grateful to see Eagle. He tried to

cheer himself, but the bitterness niggled him. He should have stopped her, but she was a Sioux and such was her way. Deveau had not beaten and tortured him. She had avenged all his transgressions and abuses, all but Murdock, and he paused to wonder for a split second, where was that devil?

Then Slocum tossed his blankets and pack on Eagle's back. Doe stepped in, moved him aside, and cinched the horse for him.

"We have the horses. Are you not pleased?" she asked as he finished the job and tucked the leather latigo in place.

"Yes, and I appreciate Two Moons's work. Tell him he's a great warrior. I might have died if you two hadn't come for me. If you must go to Standing Rock, I can take them back by myself. Horses and those boys," he indicated with a head toss.

"Good, we will see you a day's ride, then we will ride there."

He watched the rise and fall of her firm breasts under the new elk skin dress. Damn, he knew he had lost her. Even her urgency to return to Standing Rock he had dismissed, thinking he could some how dissuade her of that idea. But when he had let go of her forearms down there, he knew then that he would never again share her blankets, enjoy their bodies entwined. Their worlds were separate and he finally knew the truth.

Standing beside Eagle, Slocum reloaded the .44, punching out the empties, then shoved in fresh cartridges and tried to hide his deepest hurt. Worse than his leg ached, his heart felt a ton heavier as he slapped the Colt in his holster and mounted up.

Doe herded the horses up the hillside toward the mesa. Two Moons's prisoners were roped by the neck, like the Sioux always led their captives. Afoot, the two breeds hurried to keep up with his paint pony as he cat-hopped him up the face of the mountain toward the trail. Slocum looked back as the pole walls of the cabin collapsed and the black smoke boiled fifty feet high, then the winds swept it northward in a column. Deveau would never steal another horse in this life. Slocum booted the gray after them, comforted by the feeling of the light-footed horse under him.

He rode beneath the rock underhang, the gray's iron shoes clacking on the talus rocks. Twisting in the saddle, he looked to the west and the purple ranges that stretched off toward Yellowstone. *I've got your remuda back, old man, and lost her for sure this time.*

18

"Have you heard that last week the Jacksons shot my deputy Henry Clay?" Sheriff Nigh asked Slocum.

"He dead?" Slocum frowned at the lawman. What had they been up to?

"No, but he's had a tough time. Doc says that he'll be up and around in another week. What happened to your leg that you're favoring?"

"Had a run-in with a bear. My horse tried to take out a tree getting away from the bear and my leg got in the way."

"Man, everyone's had some kinda problem. Why, it wasn't a week ago some old squaw came wagging an army scout on a travois out of the Bighorns. He got up there and then he came down with the gout. His feet swelled up and he like to have died. If she hadn't been up there looking for chokecherries, he would have."

"His name wasn't Murdock, was it?" Slocum asked.

"Yeah, that was it. Said he was looking for a renegade and came down with the gout. Why, his toes were swelled up like an inflated hog's bladder. He said they hurt real bad. He must have drunk two bottles of whiskey laying out there on that travois in the street before they took him upstairs to Doc's office.''

''Guess he went back to the army?''

''Yeah, Phil Davenport took him in a wagon out there a day or two ago.'' He jerked his thumb toward the cell in the rear of his office. ''Well, I can guarantee those two won't get away again. I've got new chains and padlocks to shackle them up with. That damn Deveau picked the lock on the door and they got off slick as a gut on me.''

''I sure was shocked when they came and stole my horses again.''

''Good thing they did. Why, you're better than my deputies at rounding them up.''

''His squaw cut Deveau's balls off,'' one of the bucks said from the cell, pointing accusingly at Slocum.

''What the hell is he talking about?'' the sheriff asked with a frown.

''I think they both are crazy. Hell, I ain't got no squaw. They ain't been right since they tried to shoot their way out with me.''

''I can see that. Saved Wyoming some time and money not bringing Deveau back. He got his deserves. Shut up, you two, or I'll do something like that to you.''

Slocum wanted to smile at the two rustlers as they looked at each other and then hastily retreated to their bunks. It looked like they were trying to get back as far back in the cell as they could.

''Squaw, hmm.'' The sheriff rubbed his jaw as if thinking about the matter. ''I guess all of our squaw-chasing days are over.''

''I guess so. I've got cattle to check on. They're maybe scattered to Hell and back by now.''

''Good luck and thanks. You ever need some work, call on me. I could use a man like you.''

On his way out, Slocum stopped at the first saloon and bought three bottles of rye. With his purchases safely wrapped in sack towels inside his saddlebags, he mounted up and started for his camp. Standing in the stirrups, he set Eagle on a long trot.

All he had to do was push the strays up and be certain that the old man's stock was settled back on the range. In another six weeks, Crawford would be up there with the hands and they could round them up and Slocum would collect his pay. No more rustlers, old Murdock laid up with gout, Doe gone forever—why, he could heal his sore leg and enjoy the remaining time riding good horses across the Powder River country. He needed some time to think clearly anyway.

Before the first snows of winter flew, he would be turning a pony's nose south toward Texas, New Mexico, maybe Sonora. His blood was too thin to sleep by himself in some snow-locked bunkhouse. It would be nice in the Sierra Madres during the winter. The sun found their slopes and warmed them. There was a village called Rio Vaca and a woman there named Chupa, or was it Lupie? Damn, he could recall her dancing around a sombrero, swishing her skirt and showing her shapely brown legs. He'd think of her name before he got there.

Old Man Crawford owed him enough pay that he could stretch the money out for months living in Mexico. Satisfied with his plans for the winter, he set Eagle into a short lope. Maybe he'd see an antelope or deer to shoot for camp meat. How far had those rogue steers wandered? No telling.

Then a gray buck bolted down into a draw, and he took out the rifle. He let Eagle lope along the rim until he spotted the mule deer again, moving up the far side. He drew up his horse, lifted the rifle, and then whistled through his teeth as loud as he could. The buck paused in his flight and the .44/40 roared in Slocum's arms. Eagle swung around to see the tall antlered male crumble to the ground.

"Did you doubt I'd get him, Eagle?" Slocum laughed, then pushed the gray off the hillside. Nice thing about horses. They never talked back.

He gutted the deer, threw him over the back of the

saddle, and rode home in the late rays of day. He'd look in the wagon and see if there wasn't some patching for the tent. Crawford would sure be mad as hell that he'd let someone cut down on his wall tent. Never mind that they'd missed hitting him.

He frowned at the strange horse standing hip-shot in his camp. Who had taken up residence there? Guardedly he rose in the stirrups, checking Eagle to a walk and peering hard for any signs. His right hand reached for the butt of his gun.

Then he saw her step out of the tent and straighten. It was the witch from the honyockers' train. She pressed down her short dress on her legs and then grinned at him. A grown woman didn't go around wearing a dress that only came halfway to her ankles. She was hardly an inch taller than five feet, he guessed. That made her look younger. What did she want?

"Howdy," he said, stepping down and taking off his hat. "What can I do for you?"

"Oh, nothing," she said, and moved by him to examine the deer. "He needs to be skinned soon or he'll taste like hair." She turned up her pert nose in distaste. "But I reckon you know all about that."

"A little. I never caught your name." He set his hat back on his head, wondering why he'd even bothered to take it off for her; she had not noticed his action.

"I took some liberties," she said, holding up her right hand as she sashayed around to the coffeepot hanging on the S hook over the fire. "I made us some coffee."

"Fine, I like coffee. You have a name?" he asked, wondering if she'd even heard him.

She rushed off without answering him, and came back with two clean tin cups. Then she knelt down and reached for the pot with a cloth. Carefully she filled both cups, then replaced the pot over her fire of chips.

"I didn't use any of your wood. I saw it was scarce."

"No matter," he said, dropping to his haunches. "I've got to get some more anyway."

He blew on the steam. What was wrong with her?

What did she want from him? He had guessed her to be younger than she was. It was hard to tell her age, but she was not a child.

"What do they call you?" he said more pointedly.

"Why, you know my name." She blushed, and then giggled at her own expense as she held her hands up to hide her mouth. When her actions failed to bring a response from him, she looked at him hard.

"If I knew your name I'd never ask," he said, and began to sip his coffee.

"When I saw you ride into camp that day, I simply knew that you'd remember me. I recalled you the minute I laid eyes on you."

He closed his eyes. Games were games, but this one was getting out of hand. They said she was a witch—he'd known a few. He swallowed as he tried to bring up someone from his past. There had been so many faces, she didn't look familiar. He finished the coffee, and then went to take the deer down.

"I can't for the life of me—" Then the smell of saddle leather came to his nose stronger than the copper smell of the gutted buck as he sought to shoulder it. He turned under his burden and looked at her hard. No, she couldn't be. . . .

"Where will you hang it?" she asked.

"On those poles I have a rope and pulley." He indicated the tripod and set the carcass down to hook it up. She handed him the ends, and he stuck a stick in the hind-leg tendons, fastened the rope, and then pulled the deer up.

His skinning knife was stropped across the stone, and he began separating the hide from the blue carcass. He was pleased the hide came free easily, for that meant the animal was fattening. She helped pull the skin back for him, her small fingers gripping it and making it easier for him to slice. They exchanged few words, which suited him fine, as they worked. The sun was almost set over the distant Bighorns when he finished.

"I need to go get some water to wash him down good.

There's a spring over the ridge." He waited for her reply as she went for more coffee for them. His hands stank of deer guts and hide.

"I will go with you," she said. "First, here is your coffee."

It was still piping hot. He wondered if he should find a lamp. It would be dark when he got back. Twilight might not last that long. No sense breaking their necks. He handed her the cup.

"I'll get a light to see with when we come back."

"If you need one," she said after him.

Need one? Hell, he wasn't an owl. Maybe she could see in the dark—no telling about a witch. He'd never seen her before, he felt certain now as he dug out the candle lamp from the chuck wagon. Then he gathered some canvas buckets to bring back water in. With the rope handles on his arm and the metal ring of the lamp in his other hand, he headed back.

"There's water in the barrel," she said, giving him his coffee.

"Good," he said.

"It's full."

He frowned at her. No one ever filled the barrel unless it was right by the source. How long had she been there?

"Sure appreciate that," he said, and they set out for the spring.

"Prairie flowers are a-blooming again," she sang in a powerful voice that surprised him as they walked up hill. "Their flowers kissing the sun, washed by the rain, and they're waving at the passersby that they'll be back again. Oh, the prairie flowers are a-blooming again."

They washed their hands and face in the cool tank. He considered sending her back and then taking a bath for himself, but he dismissed the notion. She might not leave. So he filled the buckets, and the twilight was still good enough to see by. She carried a half-full bucket and the lamp.

"We better cook us some supper. You hungry?" he

asked. Be nice if he knew her name. Maybe if she stayed, he'd give her a pet handle. She acted like she knew him fine.

"Good idea," she said, acting pleased.

He washed down the deer while she busied herself stoking up the fire. Finished, he carved off some loin steaks and delivered them to the chuck table.

Acting at home, she busied herself flouring them. He went and poured himself some more coffee, satisfied that she could handle it. Had she lost all her folks?

"Will you light the lamp?" she asked. "It's getting dark now. I can't see what I'm doing making these biscuits."

"For hot bread I'd do about anything," he said, and struck a lucifer to the candle in the reflector behind the glass. He hung it up and then stepped back. "How's that?"

The glass shattered and he heard the rifle's distance blast as he took her to the ground.

"Oh, Gawd, Jesse! Those Indians have my baby! Do something!" She began to squall out loud and fight him as he tried to hold her down. Her legs were thrashing as he tried to keep her down and at the same time listen for hoofbeats. Finally he cupped his hand over her mouth and strained to listen. The hoofbeats were going away.

"Dammit!" she cried, tears streaming down her face. "My baby, they have it! Oh, please do something!"

"Easy, honey. They haven't got it," he said, half sick with dread. Whoever had shot at them had triggered off some bad experience in her fragile mind. He had to grasp her in his arms to keep her from jumping up and pursuing the long-gone savages. Who in the hell wanted him dead?

"Cry some," he said as she sobbed on his chest.

With her cradled in his arms, he rocked her back and forth as she cried and mumbled about Jesse and the baby. He needed to find out who had shot at them and why. Five hundred steers to look after and a woman half out of her mind—what else could happen to him next? That shooter better make some distance. *What was he up to anyway?*

19

"You find anything out there?" she asked, looking bleary-eyed as she sat by the campfire.

"No. Whoever did it is gone."

"They'll be back."

"You sure?" he asked.

"They always come back shooting and screaming."

He sat down as she dished up a plate of food for him.

"I meant to make biscuits," she mumbled.

"We were lucky that he didn't put a hole in the Dutch oven. We can have them again sometime, your fry bread's fine." He took the plate of food she handed him. Then he saw she wasn't fixing herself any food. "Get you a plate."

"But my baby . . ."

"If it's out there, we'll find it come first light. You've got to eat." He looked at the dark sky for help.

"I don't think I can."

"You better or I'm feeding you."

"You don't have to act mean to me. A mother has a right."

"Eat."

"You ain't very comforting." She sniffed.

"Where did those farmers go? Mayfield and them?" he asked between bites. Maybe they would take her back; they'd brought her out there. On second thought, they were probably glad that *he* had her instead of them.

"Who?" she asked, blinking her eyes at him. "I never heard of a Mayfield. What farmers?"

"The ones I sold the steer to after the Indians killed their ox."

"He must have died in the raid too." She looked at him blankly, nodding her head.

"He must have," Slocum agreed, and busied himself eating. She made as much sense as nothing at times.

He took their dishes and stuck them in a dishpan of hot soapy water. She hadn't said much that made good sense since they'd started to eat. He wished somehow she would get things straight in her mind, but obviously she had been through some sort of hell.

He finished doing the dishes, and discovered the water barrel full to the brim when he filled the hot-water kettle. He looked around for her. She had gone into the tent, and soon came out dressed in a thin white nightgown that hid little as she stood in the firelight. Brushing her shoulder-length brown hair, she looked as content as when he had ridden up. Maybe she was back to being herself.

He drew in a deep breath, dried his hands on the flour sack, and went to see what would happen next. She smiled at him as if they were long-time lovers. Her pink nipples showed through the thin cotton material as she brushed away at her hair.

"We going to build here?" she asked.

"I haven't decided."

"It will be fall soon. It will get cold up here."

"Oh, don't nag me, honey," he said to dismiss her, and sat down at the edge of the fire ring. Was she someone else? He tossed a small split piece of wood on the fire. What would he do with her? What if she told the authorities he had used her against her wishes? Would they believe her? There had to be a place for her where she wouldn't hurt herself and someone wouldn't hurt her. She needed help, more than he could give her. Then, deliberately, she dropped the hairbrush in his lap, and when he looked up, she was taking the gown off over her head.

He closed his eyes. Sweet Jesus, what should he do?

"Terry," she whispered, and then snaked herself into his lap. Her hands sought his whiskered face. He leaned back on his hands. Maybe she would realize he *wasn't* Terry.

"There's no one here but us," she said. "We can do what we want, can't we?"

"I'm not in the mood."

"Oh," she said with a sly smile. "I bet I can get you in the mood." She raised up a bit and her right hand sought his crotch.

"Honey, let's not. I'm upset about the shooter." His first instinct said to run, but with her in his lap, there wasn't a hell of a lot he could do but endure her.

"But you said yourself they never even shot the Dutch oven."

"I've got to get up early and check steers."

"Well," she said, her hand inside his fly, running over his privates, "you sure aren't a steer tonight. Let's go to our bed."

She was on her feet trying to drag him to the tent that formed a bright white A in the campfire's light. He finally let her pull him to his feet and inside the flap. With his head bent so he could stand up inside, he toed off his boots as she unlatched his gunbelt in a wild pull that reminded him of girthing a spoiled horse. The belt closed in tight on his belly until she undid the buckle's tongue.

When would she go mad? When would she change her mind and be someone else? She stripped his shirt off, and then his underwear to his waist. Then she hugged him as if to savor his closeness.

"Oh, I have been waiting so long for you to return," she said.

"Yes," he said. Only his name wasn't Terry. Should he tell her? Damn, he felt like some sort of aggressor taking advantage of a crazy woman in her worst time.

She pushed down his pants, and he looked at the tent's peak for help. It was beyond any stopping—when would she change to another person?

"Come down here," she said, dropping to the bedding and pulling him after her.

On the ground, he sat beside her for a long moment. She tapped him on the shoulder and indicated she wished him to lie down. The cool night air made him shiver and made goose flesh on his skin as he watched her lying on her side in the dim red light of the fire. He drew a blanket over them and lay down facing her. She had both hands folded under her face, and her green cat eyes glowed as she looked at him.

"I'm not Tanyah," she said.

"Good," he said, a shudder of relief going through his body. Her short fingers fondled him, and he wondered who she was as she scooted closer to him. Her other hand placed his right hand on her pear-shaped breast, and his heart ran away.

"You knew I wasn't Tanyah," she whispered. Then she leaned toward him and her sharp teeth bit his shoulder. Her fingers enclosed his root.

"Sure," he agreed, out of breath as her pumping fist drew him to a painful hardness. He'd agreed to anything—crazy or not.

"I need you!" she cried out loud, and rolled over on her back, pulling him after her.

He closed his eyes and let her handle the insertion as he moved down on her. On his guard, he slowly began to plunge through her slick gates. Her short legs wrapped around him, and her contractions began to pull on him with a power that dazzled him. His restraint gone, he sought her deepest source.

"Yes, yes," she mumbled, and rocked on her back,

clutching him as her waves trapped him deeper. His lungs were about to burst and his heart was running wide open. Then they both exploded and stars cascaded before his tight-shut eyes like comets filling the sky. At last they turned on their sides, locked in each other's arms, still as one, and sleep swept him away. He clung to her.

"There's a man here to see you," she announced. He opened his eyes, confused, and saw her dressed in a long blue calico dress and leaning inside the tent flap. It was daylight, and he wasn't sure whether he'd been drunk, sleeping, or what.

"Tell him I'll be right out." Slocum hurriedly dressed, his leg better but still sore.

"He was up late last night," she told whoever was out there. "He's been working hard keeping these steers gathered up. Lots for one man to do out here."

"Yes, ma'am," the man said in a Texas drawl.

"Morning," Slocum said, coming out and combing his hair back with his fingers.

"I met your wife Evelyn," the man said. "Slocum, I've got a business proposition for you or your boss."

She knew her name? She called herself Evelyn? Who in the hell was she? And where had she gotten that dress and apron? And who was this man in the suit and expensive white hat?

"Didn't catch the name." Slocum squinted and adjusted his waistband, knifing in his shirttail with a flat hand.

"Ralph Sled. I'm a cattle buyer, and someone in Buffalo mentioned that yours were for sale."

"They belong to Old Man Crawford and I'd have to wire him in Texas."

"How many head?"

"Close to five hundred."

"Good. Would eighty bucks a head buy them? She said you had five hundred head." He bobbed his head as if the amount suited him.

"Sounds to me like the cow market took a big boost

since the last time I checked on it.'' Slocum rubbed the back of his neck.

"I have some contracts that need to be filled in the next two weeks. Your cattle look in good shape and like what I need. To be honest, some of the others haven't done that good this summer, and frankly, I need some with lots of condition on them.''

"Here's some coffee.'' She handed Slocum a cup and refilled Sled's.

"I bought some cattle under that price last spring,'' the man continued. "I'll lose money on yours, of course, but in the end I'll make some money from the deal if I can deliver all of them on time. And if I fill the whole contract.''

"If I wire the old man . . .'' He tried to imagine getting Sled an answer back in two weeks. "No way.'' He shook his head.

"I need them to be in Fort Robinson in two weeks.''

"I'm maybe short twenty head.'' He wanted to level with the man.

"Trail loss. When can we make the deal?''

"I haven't seen the color of your money.''

"You want cash?'' Sled blinked.

"I'm not letting you have them on your good name, sorry.''

"If I'm back here in two days with my crew and a substantial down payment and the rest of the money at Fort Robinson, can we make a deal?''

"Yes.'' Crawford would have to like the high price. He'd never heard of any Indian beef contract that was over sixty-five dollars a head. So this man would lose fifteen on five hundred. He'd probably bought the rest for thirty in the spring, so the difference on all fifteen hundred head would make him well off.

"I have food,'' she announced, and indicated the kettles.

"You certainly are lucky to have such a lovely wife willing to stay out here all summer. Why, mine wouldn't leave Fort Worth for a million dollars.''

"I'm lucky to have Evelyn," he said, wondering when her next change was due. Thank God she'd been in a presentable condition when Sled had ridden up. Maybe Slocum hadn't slept but a few hours in the past week chasing those horse thieves and bringing in those two bucks, but still, he could never recall ever sleeping so late in years.

"I'll be back here with a crew. Would you ramrod them to Fort Robinson? You won't have a thing to do here. Why, I'd rent that wagon and send up a team. Maybe your wife would agree to cook. Make you two some extra money, since I reckon you'll be out of work when the summer's over."

"I can cook for them," she said, and wrinkled her nose at his frown.

"I'm not—" Slocum began.

"Oh, he's just afraid I'll overdo myself," she said as she saw about filling their plates.

"I'd sure think a woman cook would keep them cowboys pleased," Sled declared. "For sure over some second-rate one I'd find up here."

But maybe, mister, he wouldn't be crazy either. Slocum had a sinking spell trying to figure out how to get out from under the deal. But nothing he could say would make a difference; she had Sled in the palm of her hand. A two-week cattle drive and her a ticking alarm clock ready to go off—he could hardly wait.

But what could he do? Then she winked at him as if they had made a great deal as Sled went for his horse.

"The old—I mean, Mr. Crawford will like the sale, won't he?" she asked under her breath.

"Oh, yes. But I wish you'd let him get a cook for this deal," he pleaded under his breath.

"Why, Slocum, honey, you know I can cook for those boys." She said it loud enough that Sled heard her, and so the man grinned and tipped his hat to her.

"Mister, when you get to a telegraph office you better wire my boss," Slocum said to him. Then he went for a lead pencil and some paper from the wagon. He wrote in his best penmanship:

Macavoy Crawford, Parkerville, Texas
Sold steers for profit. Deliver to Fort Robinson, Nebraska. No crew needed. Meet me there in two weeks. Slocum.

He handed the note to the man. Crawford would hate the Macavoy business, but that was his given name. Slocum had a sickening feeling of dread in his gut about facing the man, but how mad could Crawford be over such a sale? And him not out any roundup expenses either. Oh, well, there always would be some sort of grief. Two weeks and he'd be a free man. Then he noticed *Evelyn* busy doing dishes.

"I'll send this wire to him when I get to Buffalo," Sled said, waving the paper and breaking Slocum's train of thought.

"Good. I'll start gathering them in today."

"Sure will help. We need to head them there and keep the weight on them, but you know that. Thanks." Sled touched his hat and rode off on his big roan steel-dust horse.

Slocum scratched his head. What next? And what should he do about her? His shoulders gave a small tremor under his shirt. Then she had his arm in the crook of her arm and dragged him to wagon.

"Could you fix that fly and I'll need—" Her words fell off him like rain from a rubber slicker. My gawd, he had found himself a monster. Maybe he had gone mad too, out here all summer with these cattle and Doe. Had Doe simply been a dream too? He felt his forehead for a fever, then wiped the grit off on the tips of his fingers. Someone needed to save him.

20

He looked across as she topped the coulee following a dozen head of stock. She waved and then brought Brownie over at a lope to meet him. He counted the steers while standing in the saddle.

"How many, Boss?" she asked.

"Close to fifty head, but these are the easy ones," he said as he settled in the saddle.

"I'll miss doing that when I'm working the chuck wagon," she said, looking ahead as if she was checking for one of the bunch to break.

"You ever cooked for a crew before?"

"No, but how hard can it be?"

"Damn hard work cooking for a whole crew."

"How many hands is he sending?"

"Oh, it'll take a dozen to get them there in two weeks."

"More bread, more beans, more meat." She shrugged away his concern.

"How did you ever get out here anyway?" he asked in disgusted defeat.

"Well, you should know," she said with her hands on her hips looking defensive at him. "You're the one brought me."

"I guess I did," he said, looking at the sky for help. She'd been Evelyn all day, but what if some little thing set her off. She was a little bossy, but he could stand that if she'd just be Evelyn for two whole weeks; then he'd find her a place where she could get help. They had places to help people like her—he didn't know where, but they had them somewhere.

Sled didn't come with the supplies or the five cowboys he'd sent, seven short of a crew. While gathering cattle at midday, Slocum spotted the remuda coming. He'd already sent her back to start cooking, for he felt certain the crew would arrive soon. If Sled wanted his cattle delivered on time, they'd better come soon. Then he saw them.

Maybe there had been a mistake, for the color of the horses made him think that they were rejects from an Indian camp herd. Most were paints. He could see five riders, and drew a deep breath.

"Heaven help us if this is all there is," he said out loud, seeing several of the horses carried packs. This couldn't be all the help the man had sent him to drive five hundred head.

"You Mr. Slocum?" the oldest of the hands asked, looking pained as he squinched up his left eye. "Zeke Bismark's my name."

"Slocum will do, Zeke. Where's Sled?" he asked, still looking at the stock.

"Oh, he ain't coming. He had to see about the other cattle, but he sent a bank draft for five thousand dollars," the thirty-year-old cowboy said, and dug it out of his front jeans pocket.

Slocum studied it carefully. It looked real enough, but it wasn't cash, and he wasn't taking a damn paper for them at Fort Robinson. He put it in his vest pocket and looked up and down the line at the boys Sled had sent.

Farm boys. They wore cheap round-top felt hats. Jeans so new they'd fit two slim-hipped boys at a time until they were washed or the owners forded a few rivers. Brogans for footgear. He had himself some real drover material.

"This here's Doug," Zeke said.

The slick-haired teen, who even at twenty paces smelled like Rose Oil, removed his hat and nodded. "Nice to meet you, sir."

"That's Red Baker next," Zeke leaned forward and used his thumb to indicate the freckle-faced boy with a wide grin who removed his hat and then held it up to his chest as his knuckles turned white holding the white-yellow-pattern paint back from running off.

"Glad to be here, sir."

"That's Clem," Zeke said, indicating the next dark-eyed boy, who simply nodded and sat his horse looking out across eastern Wyoming.

"Nice to have you, Clem," Slocum said, leaning on the horn as he appraised them.

"Marty Jones on the end."

"Yes, sir, and proud to be here." He was the youngest and he beamed.

"Good. Any of you ever drive a herd of cattle?"

Zeke nodded. The rest shook their heads. Slocum considered them; he needed two experienced swing men—he had only one with any experience at all. He dropped his gaze. Those spay-footed ponies weren't shod, and he had no time even if he had enough nails and shoes to do that many.

"Marty, you are the horse wrangler and you help my . . . *wife* at the wagon."

"Yes, sir."

"Zeke, you tell Marty how to keep them bunched and bring them in. Take them packs on to camp. You'll find our setup over this rise to the north. The rest of you can help me." He reined Rough around. "One thing. We ain't Banchee Indians, these cattle ain't milk stock, and they'll run off if you chouse them. Am I understood?"

"Yes, sir," came the chorus.

"Did Sled say anything else?" Slocum asked Zeke as he scratched through the long hair on the back of his neck and tried to reason out his course.

"He said it was two hundred miles to Fort Robinson."

"I'd bet it was closer to three," Slocum said, voicing his thoughts out loud.

"I've never been there," Zeke said.

"I guess we can find it. It's southwest of here. Go ahead and take care of the horses and supplies." He drew in a deep breath. He frowned at his next discovery about his remuda. Some of the horses were even mares. No one ever used mares for saddle stock. He shook his head in disgust. Either Sled couldn't find better horses, or these were too cheap to pass up buying. He'd settle with him in Fort Robinson whenever he got there. Sending four kids not dry behind the ears and one drover— why, the last one might not have even be weaned. *Old man, this job has turned into a disaster.*

"All right, we're making a sweep," he said. "Doug, you ride west, say, five miles in a circle. Then pick up any cattle you find and ease them this way. Clem, you ride south that far and bring them in here. Red, you go east, and we want to converge right here with what we find. Don't chase them if you don't have the advantage."

"What's that?" the slick-haired one asked.

"On the horse stock you all have, stay back and on the ridges. If you close in on these cattle, they'll break and run. To tell you the truth, I don't figure that on those ponies you all are riding—why, you couldn't outrun a three-legged cat."

"What if they won't come?"

"We'll get them tomorrow. Everyone savvy?"

"What's savvy mean?" Red asked with a pained look on his freckled face.

"Understand in Messikin."

"Oh, yes, sir."

"Trot, don't run, them sorry ponies or they'll die on you."

So his cowboys were sent out. His only hope was his own good success so far. The cattle acted ready to be gathered and moved. Some were coming in unaided, no doubt hearing the bawling of the ones he'd driven in and anxious to join them. Heavens, they'd been driven two thousand miles to get there. They ought to have some herd sense. But they were still longhorns, and they'd spent a big share of their lives hiding in the live oak thickets of south Texas too. Damn sure not milk stock like he figured these boys had been handling.

He set Rough in a trot. He rode north and drew in some blacks and brindle-stripped ones. They moved rather obediently, and he kept wide finding some others to add. It might take two more days to get them all in. He had hoped for experienced hands and plenty of them. Instead Sled had sent him boys. Somehow he'd get there. *Two hundred miles!* What map had Sled used? Why, it had to be closer to three hundred. The man was more fine hat and clothes than drover, and that rascal knew that somehow Slocum would get them to Fort Robinson as he'd promised or die trying. Damn his slippery hide!

In late afternoon, he could hear the others coming. A large herd came single file into the wide swale. From the east and behind him, Red came in on his yellow pinto. It was choked off by the bit until the horse's head was in Red's face as he came trotting in with his steers.

"I might not have gone far enough," the youth said, still holding the paint's head up.

"You did good. You ever let go of the reins?" Slocum asked.

"No, sir. He bucked a lot when I first got on him. He threw me three times, and I ain't letting him do that again. Made me kinda sore."

"Maybe now he's broke?"

"I don't think so." Red made a pained face.

"You did good," Slocum said, deciding that he

wouldn't change the boy's mind about the horse or how he held him.

Doug appeared, standing in the stirrups, working the cattle he brought in like a cow dog. First to one side and then the other, as the new cattle milled into the herd and some of them fought in a clack of horns. Social order, Slocum called it. Every time you brought them together, even steers had a pecking order to be established all over again. He wanted most of that out of them before they set out.

"Is Clem a good rider?" Slocum asked, not seeing the last one out on the horizon.

"Yes, sir," Red said. "He's an orphan. He's been raised from pillar to post. Don't say much, but he's a worker."

"Want me to go look?" Doug asked as he loosened his cinch and let his piebald blow. The long black and white hair on his mount was wet with sweat, and it dripped from him. "He's soft, ain't he?"

"They all looked soft to me," Slocum said, wondering why the last rider wasn't showing up. "I better go find him. You boys move this bunch northeast. You'll find the camp, ease this bunch in the herd, and then you can unsaddle and rest."

He trotted Rough south, looking across the rolling grassland. Where could one cowboy go? Had he lost his way and gone off somewhere? No telling. Had his horse fallen and pinned him under it?

Then he saw someone wave on the furthest horizon. He squinted to make the boy out as he put Rough in a lope. Clem was on foot and looked like he was shouldering his saddle.

"What happened?" Slocum asked, reining up short.

"I never run him a foot."

"What happened?" he asked as the boy slung the saddle down.

"He just went, ah, laid down and died."

"You get all your things?" Slocum asked.

"I never run him."

"I believe you."

"Good."

Slocum reached down for him to hand up his kack.

"Let me warn you," he said with the saddle situated in his lap. "This horse ain't never carried double and we may have a war."

"No problem," Clem said as he took Slocum's arm and then put his foot in the left stirrup he'd emptied for him; Slocum slung him up behind.

Rough didn't disappoint him. He went to crow-hopping off through the grass, and Slocum fought his head. Clem stayed like a tick, and when the worst of the storm was over, the boy leaned forward.

"You believe me, don't you, that he up and died?"

"I do. Don't most folks believe what you say?"

"No, sir, but you can take his cost out of my pay."

"Hell, no!" Slocum shouted as Rough had another high-pitching fit.

Seated in the grass on their butts, both of them looked at the cow pony standing with his reins trailing a few yards away. Slocum clapped the boy on the shoulder.

"Sled can buy that one. He should never have bought them sorry devils in the first place."

"Yes, sir."

"Let's go gather him up and try again," Slocum said, brushing off the seat of his pants as he rose and went for the horse. *This cattle-drive business may be the death of me, old man.*

21

"What happened, Clem?" Red ran to meet them as they rode in double.

"His horse died," Slocum said as Clem slipped off Rough and then took his saddle from Slocum.

"Oh, my God. Did you run him?" Red asked.

"No, the horse just expired," Slocum said to settle the matter for the upset youth. He looked around for the woman. "Anyone seen—"

"Well, it's about time you got back," she said, coming from behind the wagon. "These boys must be starving, they've had no lunch, but you didn't seem to worry about that. They left Buffalo before dawn."

"Feed them good then," he said, and went to undoing his latigoes.

"I'll do that, Boss Man," Zeke said.

"You're a hard taskmaster, Slocum," she said, and stirred away in some big pot when he joined her. "I cooked for a dozen. Are there more coming?" she asked him as he used his kerchief to handle the coffeepot and fill a cup.

"This is the whole crew, they tell me." His words drew nods from the four older hands. "Except Marty is out with the horses."

"But they're only . . ." A pained expression crossed her face as she looked him in the eye.

"Only boys. Say it out loud. They know it. But somehow, if you can fill their craws with food and that ragtag remuda he sent for them to ride holds up, we should some day get to Fort Robinson with these cattle, Evelyn."

"It seems to me—"

He stepped in and hugged her shoulders. "You've done very good. There's plenty of food here and someone can go out and replace that horse wrangler in a little while so he can eat."

She shrugged, went to dishing out food on the first plate, and then looked for someone to take it. They didn't need a second invitation, and when she motioned for them to go ahead, they did so with gusto.

"Plenty more to eat, so help yourself," she said, bringing Slocum a platter where he had sat on the ground to wait his turn.

"This ain't going to be easy, is it?" she asked guardedly.

"Will we do it?" he asked, taking the plate.

"I don't want to know," she said, turning her face away. "I seen some crosses and I quit thinking about it." She pushed a handful of apron to her mouth to silence her lips. "I don't want to bury them."

"I won't ask you to. And I'll do my best to get them there alive," he said under his breath. "All of us."

She knelt by him and buried her face on top of his shoulder. "Ain't no turning back, is there?"

"Nope."

"We've got to go on, don't we?"

"Yes."

"No matter what comes?"

"Can you do it?"

"I'm trying."

"Then you start acting happy and not draw these boys down. This is a big thing for them, this drive and the job. And it is a big job. They'll be men in short order. Clem lost his horse today. Laid down and died. He wanted to pay for it. He didn't think that I'd believe he had not run it. It was a first step to growing up. They'll do a lot of it. I can't protect them every hour, but I'll do my best."

"Yes," she said, and drew herself up. "Plenty of seconds," she announced as she carried her dress hem in her hand and went back to the camp circle.

He let the saliva fill his mouth. The deer meat and fresh vegetables were good. A change from dried beans and his own bland cooking—she must use salt and pepper in hers. Red soon went to replace the horse herder, and Slocum smoked a cigar as he considered the next day.

"Any of them horses in that herd stout enough to pull that chuck wagon?" he asked when Zeke came over and squatted on his boot heels.

"Couple part Percherons in there, got feathers on their feet. They're suppose to be for that. Mr. Sled said they were the team."

"He wouldn't know a draft horse from a prairie dog," Slocum said in disgust. "Who's the best driver?"

"Clem's driven horses for folks around town. Why?"

"Come morning, we're going to see how broke them plow horses are. We need to take that wagon along if we want to eat." He arched his stiff back and worked on his sore leg with both hands. The last time Rough threw him he'd landed wrong, and he'd be hurting in the morning. All he needed.

"I'll gather them before breakfast," Zeke said, and then he rose. "Tell the missus that we all appreciated her cooking and concern for us."

"Concern?"

"Yeah, she asked those of us that rode up if our mothers knew we were out here."

"She's different," Slocum said. "I'll tell her that they do."

Where had she gone? He saw no signs of her. The other boys were washing and drying the dishes for her. Marty, the kid, was seated cross-legged on the ground, eating like he was starved, and waved a spoon at Slocum between bites.

He stepped to the tent and heard her sobs. She lay face-down on the blankets. He wondered what he should do? Had this turn of events sent her back to being Tanyah? He knelt beside her and patted her back.

"What's wrong?" he asked.

"It's those three crosses I saw," she sobbed, and then threw herself in his arms. He hugged her trembling form. The wetness of her tears soaked through his vest. Who were they for? A witch didn't know everything—but they usually knew enough. Whose were they?

Zeke had the first draft horse snubbed up close to the horn as he dragged the head-slinger to camp. Oh, he would make a great draft horse in Hell. Slocum closed his eyes to the sight of the shafts of orange light that lanced across the horizon. About then the big black tried to buck on by, but the rope held and Zeke reined up to give Slocum a pensive look.

"If he was broke to drive, he's forgotten it," the cowboy said.

"Amen. The other one that wild?"

"I haven't got a rope on him yet," Zeke announced.

"Couple of you boys take the lariat from Zeke and don't let that pie-footed black devil step on you." He shook his head in disgust as she brought him a cup of coffee.

"With that horse a part of my wagon team, I may get to Fort Robinson before you do." She laughed to herself and then went off hurrawing him until she had the boys in on her joke as they anchored down the lariat in a standoff with the wall-eyed black.

"It ain't funny. Clem, go get a collar! We're breaking him to drive!"

"We are?"

"Damn right, and we ain't got time for niceties." Clem accepted Slocum's word and ran for the chuck wagon. Slocum took off his jumper and worked his way up the rope toward the wide nostrils that blew like a great fire-spouting dragon. After three tries, he managed to blind the animal with the jacket, and while that took most of the war out of him, he continued to snort under the cover as loud as before and stamp his platter-size hooves with the white feathers around his hocks.

The second horse, a deep bay Zeke delivered on the end of a lariat, was less of a fool, though he did dance a lot when the boys harnessed him.

"Anyone ever see them worked before?" Slocum asked his crew.

The head shakes were obvious.

"They bluffed out the last owner," Clem said, ducking inside under the tamer horse's head and resetting a snap to suit him. The wild one still had the jumper thrown over him.

"We hooking them up?" Zeke asked.

"Nope, let them stand and you all go eat some breakfast," Slocum said, seeing her with her hands on her hips looking impatient with him. He gave the horses a last look and then went to eat too. The black was still snorting under his cover, his blowing reverberating out his nose.

Hell, old man, things get deeper and deeper as I go. Got me breaking plow horses to drive now. She handed him a plate full of food, and he took a place on the ground.

"You ever break any horses to drive, sir?" Red asked.

"I've broke some cow ponies to a buckboard going to town. They wasn't big as these are, though. I also had a turn or two at mules. They're worse. Any of you ever broke any?"

"Couple teams," Clem said, and then busied himself eating. The others added a nod to verify his skills.

"What do we need to do next?" Slocum asked.

"Drive them," Clem said.

"Reckon we need a running W on them so they don't run off?" Slocum asked.

"No. Zeke can hold them back from horseback until they learn to whoa," Clem said.

Satisfied the boy knew his business, Slocum went to eating his food. She was busy making something on the work board under the fly. With flour on her hands, she looked contented enough. She was still Evelyn. He wondered when she would break under the duress. She would in time, he realized as he busied himself eating her fresh soda biscuits and thick white gravy.

"I'll go watch them horses a while," Red volunteered, standing before him. "Marty must be half dead staying up all night."

"Good. We'll break those Percherons today and then get serious about gathering cattle."

"Yes, sir."

The youngest of his outfit came in and dropped off his horse. He crossed the camp, his shirtsleeves too long and his britches a size or two larger than he needed and held up with a rope belt, and looked at Slocum out of half-open eyes. "Can I sleep now?"

"No."

"No?" His green eyes narrowed in disbelief.

"No, you have to eat or the missus will skin my hide." The youth nodded and headed for the campfire and kettles hanging on the iron rod. He saw her meet him and help him fill a plate; Slocum couldn't make out her words.

Marty came back and sat on the ground.

"Get lonely out there?" Slocum asked to make conversation with him.

"Damn coyotes howled all night." He tore a biscuit in two, then swabbed gravy on it before filling his mouth. Then he pushed up his sleeves and went for another.

"You'll get used to that."

"How long can I sleep today?" the youth asked, waiting, his next biscuit poised ready in his fingers.

"We ain't moving the wagon, so you can sleep till noon."

"When do I sleep when we move?"

"No one sleeps when we get the herd on the move."

"Oh." Then he went back to feeding himself as if he knew the answers and that was all he needed.

After breakfast, Clem gave the ends of the long leather lines a toss aside so they would drag. He stepped behind them as Slocum removed the jumper and then latched a lead rope on the black's head. Like a cat he stepped back and handed Zeke the tail to wrap on his horn.

"Here, get around," Clem shouted, and turned them to the right. The black danced, and soon had the bay doing the same. Slocum wondered if he should be mounted to help as they went prancing off across the grazed-down grass making wide circles.

Doug was talking to Evelyn and pushing his long greasy hair back. He was the lady's man of the outfit. Also a kind of show-off, but they'd all get their chance. Slocum would take him and ride out. He wanted those black rogues in the herd so they'd get acquainted.

"Doug," he called out, and the youth turned with his head high.

"Sir?"

"Toss my saddle on the gray in the pen and you put yours on that bay. We're going after about a dozen bronc critters."

"Yes, sir. See you, ma'am." Doug took off his round top hat and made a little cross-legged bow for her. Slocum poured himself more coffee, and then he straightened and scowled to himself. He gave Red an ax to replenish the wood supply. What a crew of misfits. Daylight was burning and he had work to do.

He and Doug rode out. Zeke waved to them as they trotted their horses headed east. The black's hide shone in the sun, soaked in sweat despite the little work he was doing. He was nervous and fretful, Slocum surmised. The others would have them settled down by the time he and Doug found the wild ones. He had last seen those rogues near the Powder River. He wanted them mingled in the bunch because they were sure to be the number-one mischief-makers when they got on the move.

They reached the river by midday, and Slocum saw several steers lying in the willows, chewing their cuds. They rose to stretch at the riders' approach. There was no sign of the blacks. He send Doug on Brownie upstream to bring them in while he went to look for more downstream.

About fifty head had been gathered when they rejoined, and Slocum and Doug headed them westward. There were no black steers in the lot. Slocum wondered where they had gone; his time to leave was drawing near. How many head did he have? One thing was for certain. He had plenty of them bawling around the spring so that he heard them in camp at night.

Doug took the steers to the grazing herd, while Slocum tried to make a count from the high point. It was slow and tedious, but he felt he had well over four hundred, with others coming in to join their cohorts. Then he and Doug trotted into camp to see Clem on the wagon seat driving the hitched team and the Percherons making turns and acting civilized. One thing had gone well that day, and Slocum duly noted it as such.

"Leave them in the corral and plan to work them tomorrow that hard," he said, riding up to speak to Clem. "The day after that we head out, and I need Marty and Evelyn to be able to handle them. I'll need you to help herd the cattle."

"Yes, sir."

"Can that boy handle them by then?"

Clem nodded, and checked the black as he stepped around impatiently. With his head set to the side, Slocum shrugged and then rode on up to the corral. He dismounted and Zeke stepped up to unsaddle for him.

"I looked over the horses after we got through," Zeke said as he set Slocum's hull on the nose and piled his blankets on top of it, hair side turned up to breath and dry.

"What's the verdict?"

"There's four we don't need to even take. Three are old brood mares that are close to foaling. They wouldn't last a day out there herding on them. The other is a crooked-legged yearling who isn't strong enough for any of us to ride."

"Still, the man owns them. We won't cut them out to ride, but we better deliver them to Fort Robinson. See any sore-footed ones that shoes might help?"

"Two geldings got split hooves. We might save them."

"Go catch them. I'll slap some shoes on them tonight. And Zeke, get any others that we could help. I don't know how many we have time to shoe."

The cowboy was already riding out and waved he had heard him. Slocum let out a slow breath and then went to look for the box with the shoeing supplies in it; he had stacked it off by the wagon.

"I sure hope he brings my kitchen back soon," she said, looking at him with a frown.

"Oh, hell, I'm sorry, Evelyn. Forgot all about you needing it to cook from." He met her displeased gaze, and then winked to soften her some. "Doug, you go tell them to bring the cook's things back or we won't eat before nine tonight."

"And it will all be your fault too." She turned with her dress in both hands and left him.

"Whew," he said after her.

He poured himself some coffee and studied the rose-colored clouds piling up on the distant Bighorns. Be an afternoon shower up there before dark. Tomorrow everyone needed to saddle and ride out, even Evelyn, and they needed to wind up the roundup and get under way the day after that.

She acted mad, not sad. Maybe she had forgotten her vexing concern over the three crosses. Whoever they belonged to.

22

The paint pony had his head stuck between his knees, and Red was fighting for control of the grasshopper. Red's eyes were twice their normal size as he crossed the open ground before the camp. Zeke was riding a zebra dun trying to catch up and assist him, but the paint was plowing sky and running all out at the same time.

The horse wrangler, Marty, who'd slept half the night splitting his guard with another, was riding a grey piebald, small, but needing to be reined like the Percherons. Doug had a fox-trotter in hand, Evelyn rode Brownie, and Slocum had the packhorse saddled for himself to save Eagle for the first day's drive. Clem busied himself hitching up his work team in the corral for the day's practice.

"You need us?" Slocum asked him.

The boy shook his head no. So Slocum turned the packhorse around and divided his forces to the four winds. He and Evelyn would go south. Doug and Marty west. Red on his plunging paint, along with Zeke, would head north. They were all to be back by mid-afternoon with what they found.

"I can tell you that many of these rogue steers will run off, but they soon come back if you go on with the other," Slocum said. "Don't waste your horses running after them, or we won't have horse flesh enough to get to Fort Robinson. Savvy?"

"Savvy!" Red shouted, and sawed on the paint's mouth until he took off running backwards. Everyone cheered at his success, and then two-by-two, they set out at a trot in their assigned directions. Slocum and Evelyn were the last to leave, and he finally twisted in the saddle to smile at her.

"They've got a lot of bottom," he said with pride, and then he set the stiff-gaited bay on his way south. While he leaned down in the saddle to check for fresh prints, he sent her to the high spots to see if she could spot any stragglers. The earth yielded no telltale sign, so they started back at midday. He was pleased for she acted excited and like herself, whoever that was.

The clouds on the Bighorns grew larger in the afternoon, and he wondered if they threatened to spread eastward. Maybe there would be a shower in the late afternoon.

"You need to get back to start supper," he said to her.

She bobbed her head under the wide-brimmed straw hat he'd found in the wagon to shade her face.

"Are the cattle all gone?" she asked.

"No, they're in a bunch by camp, don't you . . ." He looked hard at her. She knew where they were.

"Those gawdamn Indians," she cried, and her eyes narrowed to slits. "They took my baby. I'll kill every one of those red bastards!" Her small hand clutched the saddlehorn with such force that her knuckles turned snow white.

He rode in close and saw the flush on her face. What had triggered her to go crazy this time?

"Evelyn," he called to her. Then he shouted her name, and she blinked at him. He saw the change as she smiled as if the matter had washed away.

"I am glad I got to ride today," she said. "I know I can't do much good for you. But I like to ride with you."

He reached over and squeezed her arm. "You are a big help. Thank you, Evelyn."

She looked pleased as he waved for her to lope with him. He wondered how his boys had done. He needed to call them his crew, not boys, but it would be hard for him to remember. When he topped the rise and saw the black troublemakers in the assembled cattle, his heart quickened and he reached for her hand.

"They found them," he said, and then raced the pack-horse toward the boys to congratulate them.

That evening he shoed the zebra dun. It was a small mount, but Zeke felt it would be tough enough to count on when the others were worn down. His back aching, Slocum noticed the fresh hoof shavings and trimmings near the corral.

"You work on them Percherons' hooves today?" he asked Clem when he came by and crouched down on his shoe heels to watch him.

"Yes, sir."

"I'm not mad. I appreciate the help."

"Figured so."

"Can Marty drive them in the morning to the Powder River?"

"I think so."

"I don't want him hurt."

"He can lock the brake if they get too rowdy and they can skid it to Fort Robinson."

The other boys laughed at his words.

"We're going to take the herd as far as Powder River tomorrow," Slocum said, straightening and letting the dun's hoof down. "That's about ten miles from here where I want to cross. Easy ford, if that storm out there don't feed her a lot tonight." He motioned to the lightning flashing in the thunderheads to the west and the distant grumbles.

"We will be riding guard at night. That means only getting a half night's sleep for all of us. We'll quit midday and let them graze, then push them a ways in the afternoon." Finished with the front shoe, he dropped it and arched his back. He smiled in relief as Clem stepped in and began shaving with the knife on the dun's other hoof. Slocum's back wouldn't stand shoeing an entire remuda anymore. A half-dozen head had him stiff as a board and his leg complaining.

"I've got some apple dumplings," Evelyn announced, carrying a Dutch oven in one hand with a cloth and a big ladle in the other. Setting them down, she stood up and gazed at Slocum. He nodded his approval; a treat would be good for them.

"I'll get plates!" Red said, and ran for them.

"I've got the appetite, ma'am," Doug said.

"Good, but we need to save a mess of it for Marty. He's on first horse guard tonight," she reminded them.

"Yes," Clem said, looking up from fitting the shoe on the horse's hoof in his lap. "I'm his relief tonight."

The boys soon turned in to be ready for the big day, and Slocum sat by himself smoking a cigar, going over in his mind the things they needed to do and know. She took a place close by and seated herself. The hint of lavender soap fragrance touched his nose.

"I washed up," she announced.

"You suggesting I smell like a hog?"

"No."

The wind began to blow, and the smell of rain came on the updraft. He had worried about it blowing in and causing the herd to scatter.

"Going to storm after all, isn't it?" she asked, sounding upset about the matter.

"You afraid of storms?" he asked.

"I see him holding my baby in the lightning."

"Oh," he said, wondering if the storm would trigger her off.

"Slocum, I don't want to see him tonight," she said

tearfully as she moved over and settled in his lap. He tossed his cigar in the fire ring.

"You don't have to," he said to console her.

"Good. Take me to bed and love me."

"I'm all dirty—"

Her finger tips silenced him. He nodded woodenly and started to his feet, easing her off his lap. Then the entire western sky lighted in a blue-green flash of light. He could see the fury of the growing storm bearing down on them.

It might scatter the cattle without guards out there. Should he get the boys up? No use. They'd only wear out their horses' reserves, which the horses had so little of. No matter. He could always regather the cattle. She needed him.

Their urgent lovemaking in the blankets was punctuated by the dancing grave diggers that shattered the night. Flesh to flesh, their fury carried them from the earth's grasp. She clung to him as they sought relief in the privacy of the tent. Mumbling and crying, she screamed out names that he had never heard before, until she finally slipped off into a passion-caused faint that left her sprawled under him.

He pushed the hair back from her face, and in the flashes of illumination he saw the contentment on her face as the rain beat a drum on the tent's canvas sides. Two of her patches from the bullet holes leaked, but beeswax would fix that, he decided as he dressed and prepared to check on his crew. He wanted them to get some rest. They had Hell facing them.

"He didn't come," she said in a dry voice.

"Good," he said, and shrugged on his slicker. "I'll be back."

23

"Move them out!" he shouted with an arm wave over his head. The broken clouds overhead were moving south fast. Earlier, Marty and the wagon had left for the first day's camp. Evelyn had driven the remuda after it. They were going for the Powder River. Not far, but far enough for an inexperienced crew.

Zeke rode right swing and Clem rode left. Doug had the left flank, Red the right, and they were to fill in on drag if Slocum had to leave and help anyone; otherwise Slocum had the drag.

The steers were not unfamiliar with the system, and when Slocum watched them line out he felt better. They had not forgotten all their trail training up from Texas. This might be the saving grace for his short-handed herders. He waited until the line was formed and snaking eastward before he began using the tail of his lariat as a whip to get the laggers up on their feet and headed after the drive.

Back and forth he rode, shouting and swinging the tail of his reata at the slow ones. Soon the last one was

153

moving east, and he settled to ride after the stragglers keeping them going. Satisfied they were moving, he rode up to a high point and watched the herd snaking out over a half mile across the rolling country for the Powder. Grateful for the past night's rain holding down the dust, he dropped back to ride on the herd's heels and bring up the rear. It was normally a place of billowing dirt, and he knew for the next two weeks that would be his position, bringing up drag. But he was better suited than anyone else to that chore; besides, he had faith that Zeke could figure out what they needed to do up front.

Thank heavens the steers had not wandered far in the storm. From here on Slocum and his crew would have to bed them, then ride night guard and keep them together. He'd miss a lot of sleep during the drive. Oh, well, he finally was on the move and come late afternoon, they'd be ten miles closer using whatever mileage they wanted. Fort Robinson agency, here they come, five boys, a woman who might go sour any minute, and a veteran drover. *Old man, you better appreciate all this.*

The sooner they got there, the quicker he could get on with his own life. He booted Eagle after a slacker who was busy grazing instead of moving on. The steer lifted his head at the sight of him and trotted to save being busted again with the lariat.

The day passed uneventfully. Snaking up a long grade, the cattle looked like a freight train climbing a mountain. A golden eagle surveyed them and as he swooped, his great shadow passed over and spooked a few of the steers. Slocum watched Zeke and the zebra dun put them back in shape without incident. He settled back in the saddle, pleased with the cowboy's swift action. Another problem averted, he rode back and forth swinging his rope.

At mid-afternoon he heard Zeke's sharp whistle as he signaled to Clem to swing right so they could ease the cattle to the river and prevent them from jamming up. This was where he would learn if after all his explaining and questioning, the two understood the importance of spreading the cattle out along the bank. The temperature hadn't been high—in fact at times Slocum had felt like wearing his jumper when the clouds cut off the sun— so the stock wouldn't be too thirsty.

They'd settle in and get a drink, and then be easy to bed across the river. He was displeased with his first sight of the muddy river. The rain had raised it, but he calmed down when he saw the multicolored remuda grazing across the ford on the flats. He also saw the white tarp of the chuck wagon across the river, smoke curled skyward, and sent Eagle downhill in a head-bobbing walk.

One day down and at least a dozen more to go. The cattle should cross the river easily when they had a drink, except for the last few, who always had to be driven in any bunch. Then the riders could gather them across on the other side, let them graze, and bed them up tight for the night. No way these boys would have survived the day on their sorry horses if the steers hadn't been trail broke. Slocum felt pleased.

Once down the hill, he sent the gray horse past Doug on his paint with a high sign.

"Good job. Push them easy and we'll let them graze out on the other side before we bed them down."

"Yes, sir."

He caught Clem sitting a yellow piebald, and drew up beside him.

"We had a good one today. We need over a dozen more like them. You boys did a helluva job." Then he told him the plans.

"I thought it went all right," Clem finally said.

"Veteran Texas drovers couldn't have done better on steel-dust horses." He waved at the youth, then slanted his descent down the steep slope to hit the river and cross it downstream of the cattle watering in the river and spreading down the bank as if they were at a great trough.

He loped into camp and dismounted. She came running from the tent that she and Marty had obviously put up. He didn't care that it wasn't set up with a tight enough roof line and that the door faced the coming cattle so that the trail dust would sift in. He could see the glow on her face.

"Marty did good," she bragged. "I'm glad, though, they were big horses. The other horses all had to swim. The water got almost to those Percherons' backs at noontime when we crossed with the wagon. It's gone down a lot since then."

"One of you needs to measure these fords by riding ahead," he said with a frown. "You could have lost the wagon and supplies too."

"We know now. You couldn't tell us everything." She handed him a hot fried apple pie in a deep brown pastry that sent vapors of cinnamon up his nose.

"Right. Thanks, they smell good."

"I made everyone a treat to celebrate the first day on the way."

"Good idea," he said, then took a bite from the corner of his.

Steers with dripping bellies busied themselves grazing as they came by the camp. Zeke rode up. She ran out and handed him a fired apple pie.

"Whew! Fried pie!" he said aloud at his discovery. "Thanks, ma'am."

"Get on a horse to deliver them," Slocum said to her with a frown. "Those longhorns ain't milk cows. They might decide to chase you."

"Oh, yes, sir, Boss," she said, and hurried off to get Brownie, who was tied to the chuck wagon.

"Had a good day," he said to Zeke. "We can let them graze a couple of hours and then bed them down. May take some extra hands the first night."

"We'll do that," Zeke said, and rode on to contain them.

Slocum watched her wind her way around until each rider had his own pie. He grinned at the impressed cowboys as they held their prizes high to show her they were grateful.

"You're going to ruin them to work for any other outfit," he said when she returned.

"A little spoiling won't hurt them boys. Those horses aren't going anywhere, are they?" she asked, tossing her head to the remuda. "I sent Marty to bed so he'd be fresh for night guard tonight."

"If you could stampede those shaggy deadheads you're better than I am." He rubbed his left eye with his index finger. There was something in it besides the crust of dirt on his lashes.

"Slocum, who's out there?" she asked. "Someone's coming."

He studied the riders. One looked familiar, and he undid the thong on his Colt hammer as he wondered who was coming with him.

"Who is it?"

"One is an army scout named Murdock. The other two I don't know."

"What do they want?"

"Hell only knows. Why don't you go back up to the chuck wagon and let me handle them."

"You sure?"

"Yes, I'm sure."

"Don't do nothing foolish." She waited for his promise.

"I won't. Go back." He felt a tightening of his jaw muscles as he watched the buckskinner coming on a bald-faced horse.

What did Murdock want? The other two must be scouts with him. Even at a distance Slocum could see the man wore huge slippers on his feet, no doubt to avoid the pain of anything tight on them. The other two looked like breeds or white trash. They did not impress Slocum as any good or up to any good either.

"Two of horses in that bunch . . ." Murdock blinked and held out his arm to stop the others from riding closer to him.

"Slocum, what are you doing here?" he demanded.

"Guess that's for me to know and you to find out."

"Two of those paints in that hoss herd are mine," Murdock said as the other two looked around like a pair of buzzards looking for carrion.

"Split ears, huh?" Slocum asked

"Yeah, everyone in Wyoming knows that's my mark."

"That's what Injuns do to mark their buffalo horse. You must own a helluva lot of them."

"You denying me my horses?" Murdock demanded.

"You better shuck your guns. That Henry pointed at you from the tent is fixing to cut you down."

They fell for it and whirled to look. When they turned back they faced his Colt. Eyes wide, they raised their hands, looking at each other as if questioning how he had pulled such a trick on them.

"Shuck them irons, boys. Use your fingers easy. One wrong move and I'm venting your carcasses with lead." Slocum felt the muscles in his body tense. Three tough hardcases, and he needed to watch their every move.

"By damn, you're messing with the U.S. Army," Murdock swore.

"Murdock, this herd and those horses aren't any of the army's business and you know that."

"Let's talk here," Murdock said, dropping his Colt on the ground. The others did the same with their side arms. Marty came from nowhere and darted in and out gathering them with a wary eye on the scouts. "We're on army business here," Murdock said.

"That's what you say. Marty, you unload those that you can," Slocum said, meaning the cartridge models. "And then find a tow sack to put them in."

"Yes, sir," he said, still keeping a wary eye on the three men.

"Where's my squaw?" Murdock asked, his eyes narrowed to slits.

"Canada with Sitting Bull, I guess."

"You're lying."

"Believe what you want. Murdock, you come back,

bother me and my people, you won't ride out of my camp again except in a hearse.''

''Those are my horses—''

''They won't do you any good in Hell.''

''We'll see about that.'' Murdock started to turn his horse to leave.

''Suit yourself, but the boy's bringing them pistols back if you want them.'' Marty came lugging the sack of them from the wagon.

''Give him his irons.'' Slocum motioned toward Murdock.

''You ain't heard the last of this.'' Murdock waved the sack at him, and then gave a head toss for the pair to ride out with him. ''I catch that Sioux squaw next time, I'll cut her tendons and she won't run away from me again.''

Slocum holstered the Colt before he gunned the man down. His breath raged in and out of his nose. Before this life was over, he needed to do the world a favor and send Murdock to his reward. He'd waited too long already.

''Who are them fellas?'' Marty asked after Murdock and the others left.

''Whipper Murdock is the big one. The other whiskered bastards are his henchmen, I'd say.''

''You all right, Boss?'' Zeke asked, sliding the dun on his heels and looking warily after the three men as they rode north.

''Can you use a pistol?'' Slocum asked.

''I can.''

He drew out his extra .31 Dragoon-model Colt and holster from his saddlebags. ''It's loaded, Zeke. Don't draw it unless you need it.''

''I won't. What did they want?''

''They said some of our horses were theirs,'' Marty said with a shake of his head. ''I call them hardcases.''

''They think that,'' Slocum said, wondering when they'd try something else.

"Time to bed the herd down?" Zeke asked, finished putting the holster around his waist.

"Yes," Slocum agreed, and saw her coming from the tent. "I'll join you boys in a few minutes."

"We can do it, Slocum." And Zeke was gone.

"I thought those men would kill you," she said in a hushed voice.

"They didn't get up that early."

"They'll be back." She hugged her arms and shuddered. Then, with her eyelids narrowed, she looked off in their direction, although they were now mere specks on the horizon.

He had figured that Murdock would give him some trouble before the drive was over—he hated that she had told him that Murdock would be back. She might know something else that was going to happen to them between there and Fort Robinson. He didn't want to know what.

24

The trail drive became a routine. The wagon set out with Marty on the seat, talking to the Percherons like a mule skinner, and Evelyn drove the horse herd. They left first each morning. Sometimes they'd go more south than Slocum planned, or travel too far to reach water, and he'd have to make a short day the next day to keep the steers in condition.

"Are we any closer?" she asked one night as they lay in their blankets.

"You anxious to get there?" he said, so tired that his eyelids were like trapdoors.

"No. I want to herd cattle forever."

"I'm ready to get there."

"I guess we'll get there when we do. Strange going to a place that you've never been. There aren't any roads we make our own. What if it isn't there?"

"Trust me, Fort Robinson is out there," he said, turning over on his side with his back to her. He had to have some sleep. She snuggled her warm form against him, and he soon fell asleep.

Stampede! He was on his knees. The sound of thundering hooves and the bawling cattle filled the night. He pulled on his boots.

"What is it?" she asked.

"The cattle have stampeded."

"Be careful," she said, squeezing his arm as he rose, strapping on the .44. He rushed out and mounted his saddled horse.

"Everyone up!" he shouted to the sleepy boys. "Cattle's on the move!"

"Coming," was the chorus.

The night was dark, with the only light from the stars. He wondered what had awakened the herd. Panic would spread through sleeping cattle like a prairie fire, and once they were on their feet they ran for miles. He might lose a quarter of them running off a bluff, or they could simply run themselves to death. He sent Brownie through the dark sage, feeling the bay would know if something was afoot. An experienced trail-driving horse was like a buffalo pony. It knew. As he raced across the swale he hoped that he could see the herd soon. Doug and Clem were on guard. Where were they at? Many good cowboys were lost in stampedes. A gopher hole, prairie dog town, horse spill—anything could take them.

With the wind in his face, he finally found the trotting end of the herd. These animals had begun to lose their fervor for running. Then he turned his ear to listen and heard the chousing and shouting. In the dim starlight he could see Doug and Clem had turned them back. He reined in the heaving Brownie and thanked his Maker. Relieved, he could hear both of the boys shouting at the cattle as the herd slowed down.

"Ease up, they've got them!" he shouted as the others rode up.

"What happened?" Red asked, jerking his mount to a halt.

"We had a stampede—could have been an angry badger bit one for being on his ground. We may never know. We're lucky they weren't yearlings or fresh from the brush. We better ride around and gather all we can. We get them as best we can in this darkness. Then we can get the rest in the morning.''

''There goes our sleep,'' someone complained, and then clucked to his horse.

Sleep, what the hell was that? By midnight they had most of the cattle bedded, and he sent the first shift to the wagon. Under the stars, he rode back with the weary crew concerned over how far the steers had run.

''They just jumped up and ran off,'' Doug said in disbelief.

''You have a notion why they spooked?'' Clem asked.

''Probably never know whatever gets into a longhorn's small brain,'' Slocum said.

''I can testify that it don't take them long to get up and run,'' Doug said. ''Man, it was black out there.''

''You boys did good tonight. All of you. We were lucky.''

''Yes, sir.''

Slocum dropped out of the saddle, undid the cinch, and tied Brownie to the hitch line. He dropped across the blankets, his outflung arm reaching toward Evelyn. It fell on nothing but bedding, and he blinked. Where was she?

''Everyone all right?'' she asked from the flap as she dropped to her knees and crawled in to join him.

''All accounted for but you.''

''Someone was sneaking around camp. I went to try and see them.''

''You see them?'' he asked, wondering who would do such a thing and what they wanted. His first thought was Murdock, but he wasn't the only person in the territory up to no good. Someone could have started the stampede to test the mettle of his crew.

''No. But they were out there.''

''One or two?'' He sat up and considered what he should do.

''One for sure.''

He closed his sore eyelids. Was it all a figment of her

imagination? She wasn't the best witness in the world. Still, he would look around in the morning for any sign.

"I'll see about it come first light," he promised, and then fell back on the blankets. She covered him and then snuggled close.

At dawn they dragged themselves up. Marty caught fresh horses for everyone. Slocum was amused sipping his coffee. His sluggish remuda was no trouble to rope, not like the usual remuda that ran about ducking thrown lariats. The boy would make a hand, but the dull ponies were good for him to learn on. Slocum mounted his concern centered on the growing number of lame mounts. They had to be down to less than two rideable mounts per cowboy.

"Doug and Clem, you two make a wide sweep and try to bring in the scattered ones. The herd should stay on the ground, there's grass here. Send Zeke and Red back for breakfast. I'll catch up with you. I need to check on a few things."

"We moving today, sir?" Marty asked.

"No, there's water here in that creek over there. We may heal up for a day. Saddle a horse and ride with those boys. Them ponies aren't going anywhere."

"Yes, sir!"

"Don't that boy need some rest?" Evelyn asked with a frown as he fixed his cinch. "He's been up all night herding them horses."

"We all do. He looked happy to me to get to cowboy for a change and I need all hands."

"What about me?"

"I need you to cook, remember."

"But we aren't moving."

"You stay here."

"Yes, sir."

He rode Eagle in a wide loop around the camp. Amid all the split hoofprints from the herd passing over the ground, he did see some moccasin toe marks. Not boot prints or the shoe prints of his men, but genuine Indian prints. No telling, with his remuda half barefoot and half shod, whose horses' tracks they were.

Who had scouted their camp? Not Murdock. These footprints weren't made by big slippers, but it could have been one of his henchmen. Either one of those grubby riders that came with him could have been snooping around camp. Damn strange they came on the same night that the cattle stampeded. Or convenient anyway.

He short-loped Eagle eastward. They had cattle to assemble again. How many were missing? As he looked across the rolling grassland at the grazing cattle, he hoped not many.

25

Five days passed. Everything grew routine, and their drive became sleepless drudgery. Slocum was convinced they had lost less than a half-dozen steers. Temperatures soared, and the water they found was less plentiful, as well as mossy and tepid-tasting. He wished for the cool water from the Big horn snows, but they had enough to quench the thirst of both man and beast.

"Are we halfway?" Zeke asked as they rode back in the twilight from the herd.

"I think so."

"We ain't seen a soul but those scouts in over a week."

"I don't need to see them again," Slocum said.

"Me either."

"What if we drive by the place?"

"We won't. I expect to hit a road soon. Fort Laramie is about due south of us, and Fort Robinson should still be southeast."

"I guess we're going the way that my grandfather said he come out here, by gosh and golly," Zeke said, mopping his sweaty face as they rode.

"Must be," Slocum agreed, and they pushed on to camp. There was a hot wind in his face as he dropped down and undid the cinch.

Those not on guard slept on top of their bedrolls in the shade of the wagon. Slocum saw Evelyn pour him a cup of coffee, and he went to get it. Despite the heat, he needed something to lift him. The horses were getting more lethargic, and he wondered what he could do to rouse everyone up. They still probably had a week's driving ahead of them.

The steers' condition looked good, but in this dried country they were crossing they might lose some of that bloom. Even in a land bisected with water, a small herd could have a tough time.

"Where's Marty?" Doug asked, riding into camp on his piebald. "I need a horse for Red out there."

"What happened?"

"We were riding around the herd when his big paint just dropped in his tracks and spilled Red on the ground. Guess this blessed heat got him."

"Red all right?"

"Sure. He hated that it happened."

"Go easy on them ponies. We don't have any to spare," Slocum said, and then took the coffee from Evelyn.

"What will we do if we lose many more," she asked. "We'll be afoot."

"We will be. Between stove-up and lame ones in the remuda, we are about to become foot soldiers now."

"You said you shouldn't be on foot around these cattle."

"You can't. If we get too low, I'll ride ahead into Fort Robinson and get some more horses."

"I figured that Sled would have ridden out to meet us by now," she said. "And we don't have a strip of meat in camp either."

"What do you want? A crippled horse or a lame steer? I haven't seen a deer or antelope in two days even at a distance."

"A fat steer would be fine."

"I'll rope one and drag him in. Get them boys up. They can help skin it."

"But they haven't had any sleep," she protested with a frown.

"They can sleep the rest of their lives when we get there. Want me to wake them?"

She looked as tired as any of them. "No, you go rope the steer. I'll wake them."

Not choosy what he picked to butcher in the twilight, Slocum roped one and then dragged him from the edge of the herd. At camp, he dismounted, went up the rope, and shot the bawling critter in the head at close range with his .44. The horned son of Texas brush country went down on his knees, then flopped on his side as the life drained from him.

Zeke stepped in and cut his throat as the others brought the poles, block, and tackle. The rush of crimson spilled out on the thirsty ground as they prepared to haul him up in the air. In a short while he was skinned and gutted, his sliced liver frying in her skillet with a shredded onion or two.

The boys perked up some and ate hearty of the liver, onions, and sweetmeats as Evelyn browned some back strap for them too. Bent over the fire, she shared a wink with Slocum as she turned the meat in her pans. Numb as the rest, he nodded and chewed on his last bite.

He sent Marty and the wagon off in the early light the next morning. He kissed her tenderly on the mouth and looked deep into her hazel eyes. She looked as exhausted as the rest.

"You all right?" he asked, concerned.

"I'll be fine, except those crippled horses get slower and harder to drive. I hate to beat them." She made a distasteful face.

"Leave them behind. If they can't be used, we don't need them."

"When we started, you told the boys that they belonged to Sled."

"I said we'd take them if they weren't any trouble. These cattle are worth a lot more to him and we need to save our strength."

"I'll be fine." She forced a smile for him, but the lines around her eyes worried him.

"I hope so."

He watched her trot off to round up the remuda. Damn, they must be getting close to Fort Robinson. Or were they lost? Why hadn't Sled come out and seen about them? Two tries and Slocum was in the saddle. Zeke and the boys were shaping the herd. He looked at the cloudless sky; it would be another scorcher of a day. There had to be some summer heat. Hell, it had snowed and done everything else this season.

The day dragged on. Lightheaded in the thick dust churned up by the herd, he kept the growing number of stragglers on the move. It almost required two riders at the rear. His cow ponies were showing the wear too. A bandanna was pulled up over his nose and mouth to filter out part of the dirt in the air he breathed.

Half asleep in the saddle, he saw Red coming through the thick curtain. What was wrong?

"Zeke thinks something is wrong at the camp ahead," the freckle-faced boy said, jerking down his mask to shout over the cattle's bawling.

"What does he think is wrong?" Slocum asked.

"He wanted you to go check. Says we're close to water, but he says something's wrong. Ain't no smoke or horses in sight. I'll bring up drag. You go see."

Slocum drove Eagle out of the dust and wiped his face to clear away some of the residual dirt. Clear of the herd, he short-loped ahead. He could see the other riders swing the herd around to send them toward the creek.

There was more grass here. They had been coming uphill all day. The silver creek looked good, and he could see the wagon tarp as he loped the big gray. No smoke or horses. Something *was* wrong. Evelyn had plenty of cow chips. The boys kept the sheet full that was swung under the belly of the wagon.

Someone was lying face-down. He urged the gray on, jerking his .44 out as he slid him to a stop. It was Marty. He saw no sign of Evelyn. He knelt on the ground and rolled the boy over. Damn, there was blood all over his shirt. He held the limp form in his arms.

"I tried . . . stop them . . ."

"Who?" Slocum leaned over to hear his pained words.

"Murdock." Slocum watched the boy's blue eyes fade, and death eased Marty's pain as he cradled him.

"What happened?" Doug asked, jumping off his horse.

"I don't know. They shot Marty. Get a blanket."

"Who did it?"

"Murdock, Marty said."

"I want the son of a bitch's hide," Doug said through his teeth.

So did Slocum. His cowboys rode in and hurried to join him. He looked about. Where was Evelyn? He could hardly face the fact Murdock had her in his clutches. He tried to dismiss it. She was somewhere hiding, or off checking on the remuda. Where were they at? He looked around as he went to the wagon carrying Marty. The remuda wasn't in sight. They'd killed a boy for that sorry herd? A sickness rose in his throat and threatened to cut off his breath as he laid the boy's limp body down on the blanket Doug had spread out for him.

"There isn't a sign of the missus anywhere," Zeke reported. His tanned, dirt-streaked face was as white as the others as they circled around Slocum.

"Spread the cattle out. I want everyone to get some sleep tonight, rest their horses. Come first light, we'll go look for them. We can't do a thing in the dark but get ourselves hurt."

"How we doing the guard duty tonight?" Red asked.

"We ain't, we're all sleeping. Come first light, we're trailing these killers down."

The men nodded at his orders. Zeke handed Doug and Clem a shovel apiece.

"In that chuck wagon there should be a few rifles and some cartridges," Slocum said, fighting back the knot in his chest. Poor Evelyn. Damn, he should have killed that worthless Murdock the first day he saw him with Doe.

"There's two Winchesters and one shotgun," Zeke reported.

"Load them to the gate and hand them out. Anyone needs instruction, you show them." He wanted to be alone, by himself, but he was the leader of this bunch. They looked to him for leadership, and they damn sure needed some.

"The cattle should stay close for a couple of days," Zeke said, jamming brass casings in the repeater. "There's water in the stream and good grass."

"They should be easy for us to get them up. If we don't find Murdock in that much time, we may never. Who's the best cook of the four of us?"

"Damn, Slocum, I'm not sure," Zeke said. "But I sure can't cook nothing that a human would eat."

Slocum itched to ride after them alone. No, he had four men to take care of, and they wanted revenge too. It was Evelyn that Murdock and his bunch would hurt. Taking and abusing her might mean she never came back from being someone else. They'd pay if they did that to her. He went with the others to bury Marty.

Hats in hand, they stood in a small circle around the packed dirt mound over Marty's grave. With their heads bowed, they waited for Slocum to say something.

"Lord, we live a simple life out here," he began. "Marty come out here to be a drover and made himself a good hand. Unarmed, he was cut down by men not worth his shoe leather. Take him in your palm, Lord, and deliver him to the Pearly Gates, amen."

"Amen."

"We better make a fire and cook some grub," Slocum said, and in silence they headed back for the wagon.

His food had no taste, but maybe no one's food did. Maybe because it wasn't her cooking, but it wadded in his mouth. He finally went for the rye whiskey he had so carefully hoarded away.

"Boys, get yourself a cup. I've got some medicine we all need. Powerful stuff." He went around and filled each one's tin cup half full. "We seen some things happen made us all mad. We're resting here tonight. They ain't going fast driving that bunch of horses." He sipped some of the whiskey, letting the fire of the liquor cut the dust in his throat before he spoke again.

"Boys, I've got to warn you that Evelyn's had some serious problems in her life. I think that Indians killed her baby in a wagon raid. She's never really got over that, so I'm warning you that she might be out of her mind when we find her."

"If they've hurt her . . ." Doug said, then wiped his mouth on the back of his hand, holding the tin cup level before him.

"We're going to get her back, boys. Get them horses back. Revenge will blind you, boys, worse than this whiskey. I hate them more than you do, but I'm going to get her back and them damn paint horses of Sled's." He had to turn away.

26

They were groggy from their first full night's sleep in over a week, but in the yellow light of the peeping dawn, their saddle leather protesting, they mounted. Their hooves pounded the prairie. Five abreast, they rode north. Each man armed and ready, they followed the remuda tracks, making Slocum wonder if taking the horses was a dodge to make them leave the cattle behind. Still, they had plenty of tracks and they'd use them up first.

At mid-morning, they spotted the abandoned ponies scattered across the rolling grassland. Slocum drew his Colt and led the way in. He wondered if they had only abandoned the sore and lame horses.

"Check for the sound ones if you need a fresh horse," he said as he searched around for a sign of the rustlers.

"My dun's here," Zeke cried out at his discovery.

"Can I catch the packhorse and ride him?" Red asked. "This piebald I'm on is about done in."

"Sure, Red, catch him. Any of you boys seen Brownie or Rough?" Slocum asked, standing in the stirrups to look over the scattered horses out among the grass and sagebrush.

"No, they must have kept them."

"Clem, you ride out that way, and I'll go north, and we'll all look for their tracks."

"Sure." The youth, carrying a Winchester in his right hand, sent his split-eared mount westward.

"I'll go east," Doug said, and slapped his piebald on the butt with his shotgun barrel and loped off.

Slocum tracked through the low sage, leaning out of the saddle, looking for a sign of where the rustlers had gone. Somewhere ahead, Evelyn was still their prisoner, and her treatment in their hands ate at him. He never should have . . . but how could he have helped it? She'd come to him. It seemed now as if that had been years before, instead of only weeks.

The others had spread out and they rode about a hundred feet apart, each one intent on the ground and finding a clue to where the killers had gone.

Slocum wondered if they were good enough to find a real scout's tracks. Murdock was no fool, and he had to suspect that Slocum would come after them if he took her for whatever purpose. Either he would leave a broad track and hope to entrap him, or else—

"They went north!" Red shouted, and pointed that way.

Slocum rode over and inspected the prints. Shod horses. One of them was Brownie. Good, they wanted Slocum to follow them. Murdock figured he was good enough to meet him head on. He might not have expected this large a posse. Slocum would almost bet the scout thought he would come alone and they could ambush him anytime they wanted. *Guess again.*

He set Eagle into a long lope, and the others followed him in a hard sweep northward. Their horses' hooves pounding the ground, they went over the rise and saw the stream and the camp below in the cottonwoods.

"Let's get them bastards!" Doug shouted, and charged his piebald off before Slocum could call them off. The others did the same. He wanted to hold back, but nothing was going to stop the anger of his men.

He sent the gray charging to the front and shouted for them to spread out. Puffs of gun smoke came from the trees as the gelding plunged downhill in leaps that jarred Slocum as he fired his Colt at the ambusher behind a thick trunk.

He jerked out his Winchester and slid the gray to a stop. His first shot threw bark in the shooter's face. Then the man turned and ran. Slocum next 44/40 bullet cut the rustler down. His knees buckled and he sprawled out on the ground. Slocum turned and saw that Red was hit, holding his arm, and that Clem was riding after another rustler, who was running for his horse.

A shotgun blast shattered the air. Then the second killer screamed.

"Tell them to stop shooting!" Murdock shouted, coming from some cover near the river, holding Evelyn as a shield before him with a six-gun in his other hand. Her dress was torn, filthy with mud, and her hair hung limp. But worse, Slocum saw the listlessness in her downcast eyes.

She didn't know them.

"You no-good bastard! You better let go of her!" Red said, holding his arm, which was red with blood. He seemed about to charge Murdock without even a gun.

"Hush, boys, he's got the upper hand," Slocum said, holding his hands out to stop them from doing something rash.

"Damn right I do. Call your dogs off, Slocum. If you ever want to see her alive, you better throw down your guns and listen to me."

"What do you want?" Slocum asked.

"One of you go saddle that long-barrel bay horse for me to ride. I'll take that gray of yours for her to ride."

"Saddle him Rough, boys," Slocum said over his shoulder.

"One of you only!" Murdock ordered, and held the

muzzle menacingly close to her temple as he jerked her up.

"I will," Clem said, and ran off to capture the bay.

"What else you want, Murdock?"

"I considered killing you. Should have back there. I never figured these boys had all that much fight in them." He shook his head. "Changed my plans. I figured you'd come riding in by yourself. Guess you spooked Fargo and Nick. Damn fools. But I've still got the high card, don't I, girlie?" He jerked her up, and his action only made the cowboys start for him. She never answered him.

"You like his missus, huh?" Murdock showed his yellow teeth and grinned smugly at them.

"You got that gun, mister," Zeke said. "But next time I'll kill you with my bare fists."

"Ha, ain't going to be no next time, boy. She ain't his missus either. Never was. She's crazy, did you boys know that? Injuns held her captive for three months. I recognized her back there. The troopers brought her in to Fort Lincoln over a year before that Custer got his balls cut off. She was so crazy then that them Indians was plumb afraid of her. They won't kill her either, bad luck to kill a crazy woman. But I don't give a shit. You give me a reason, I'll kill her."

"Easy, Murdock, we're getting your horse for you. Where are you leaving her?"

"When I figure you ain't tracking me, Slocum, I'll leave her."

"Son of a bitch!" Red swore, his good hand clutching his wounded forearm and dripping with his own blood.

"Easy," Slocum said, concerned they might trigger something worse out of this madman.

"Get on that horse," Murdock said in her ear as he waved them back. He shoved her toward the gray as Clem brought the bay horse up. Numbly she mounted Eagle, and holding the saddlehorn in a daze, she swayed some as Murdock moved around trying to wave a pistol and lead Eagle close enough for him to get on the bay.

"Get back," he ordered Clem. Slocum wondered what he should do next. Then he saw the switch that Clem carried close by his leg.

Murdock swung up with some effort. Clem moved into action and with both hands holding the stick, he jabbed the gelding hard in the flank. Rough squealed like a stuck pig, and the horse left the earth for the moon. Zeke raced over and swept Evelyn from the gray. Slocum rushed for his Colt as Murdock roared like a grizzly caught in a bear trap and the pony bucked for the river.

Then the blast of a shotgun broke the confusion. Shot under the arm Murdock stopped screaming. Running beside the bronc with the smoking scattergun in his right hand, Doug reached up and tore the man's body from the saddle, and it had no more than hit the ground when he tried to bash Murdock's head in with the gun butt.

"He's through!" Slocum shouted, out of breath, pulling him back. "It's over. He's dead."

"I want to be sure," Doug said, and raised the gun butt.

"He ain't going to do anything else to anyone. You made sure of that. Go check on Red's arm."

Doug agreed, dropped the shotgun, and then ran to where Red knelt. Slocum hurried to where Zeke held Evelyn in his lap.

"She ain't in good shape." The cowboy made a face and then shook his head.

"Evelyn! Evelyn, do you hear me?"

"Terry, that you?" she asked as if awakening from a dream.

Zeke blinked his eyes and frowned as Slocum shook his head. He took her in his arms and sent the cowboy to see about Red. Damn, he hoped the boy wasn't hurt bad. He'd sure lost enough blood.

"That you, Terry?" she asked.

"We've got to go back to the cattle, Evelyn. The herd."

"Yeah, get them damn steers to Fort Robinson," she slurred like a drunk person.

He closed his eyes and breathed a sigh. Maybe in time she would be herself again. He hugged her face to his chest. Please, please let her mind recover.

"Gawdamn, Slocum, Red's fainted! You better get over here real quick!" Doug shouted.

27

"It'll take all three of you boys to hold him down,"
Slocum said as he poured the gunpowder out of another
cartridge onto the piece of white paper. The gray powder
was mounded like sand. He pried another bullet off a
casing by inserting it into a bullet hole they'd made for
that purpose in the bark of the cottonwood.

"That's the only way to treat the wound?" Red asked
with a pained face, trying to raise up from his pallet to
observe the operation.

"The bullet went through and I can't see much damage to your arm, but we need to cauterize the wound or
you're going to bleed to death."

"Whatever you say." The flush-faced youth lay back
down.

"Doug, you get on this side, Zeke on the other, Clem
hold his feet. You ready, Red?"

"I guess."

Slocum checked the others. They gave him numb
nods. He gave Red a belt to bite down on. Then, using
the paper as a funnel, he sent the gunpowder into the

179

bloody wound, forming a small pyramid of the grainy material. Then he struck a lucifer and touched off the powder. The flash blinded them. A sickening stench of burning flesh and smoke filled Slocum's nose as Red's cry shattered the silence.

The cowboy twisted and his body strained in tremors against the force of his holders. Then Red fainted. Everyone else caught their breath as they released him.

"Is he going to make it?" Doug asked, raising up on his knees.

"He's already quit bleeding. What now?" Zeke asked.

"We've got steers to deliver," Slocum said.

"Should we bury them?" Zeke asked with a head toss to indicate the rustlers.

"It's up to you, boys. Be the Christian thing to do."

"Let the buzzards pick his bones," Doug said disgustedly.

"Then you ain't no better than they were," Slocum said, looking at them for a reply.

"No." Zeke said. "We'll bury them. You go take care of her."

"Thanks," Slocum said, getting up stiffly from his knees in the sand.

He found her still sleeping in a ball on the blanket. He dropped down and sat on the ground watching her in slumber. He'd learned many things about her bit by bit. So she had lived among the Indians as a captive and they'd thought her crazy, too crazy to kill.

Time passed slowly and soon Zeke came leading Eagle and one of Murdock's horses saddled for her.

"Is she ready to go?"

"I'll wake her up after you boys ride on. Gather all those loose horses on your way back. We sure need those Percherons to pull the wagon. How's Red?"

"He claims he can ride."

"Watch him," Slocum cautioned. "He may pass out on you."

"We will. You going to make it with her?"

"I think so. I'll be in camp by dark."

"Glad this is over, aren't you?" Zeke asked with a grim set to his thin mouth.

"Yeah. I'll be more glad to get to Fort Robinson."

"I ain't. Just have to look for more work," Zeke said, and shook his head.

"You'll find some. You're all good hands. See you boys in camp."

"Oh, one more thing." Zeke stopped his remounting and turned back to face Slocum. "We found some money on them fellas before we planted them. We all wondered if we could take it back to Marty's folks."

"Good idea. How much did they have on them?"

"About twenty-five dollars." He held up a bandanna tied in a wad.

"Keep it. Sled's paying him full wages for the whole trip to put in with that."

"Good." Zeke went and mounted his pony, then rode off to join the other three. They waved to Slocum, and then he turned back to her.

"Were you going to wake me? What was that all about?" she asked sleepily. "How long have I been napping?"

"Not long enough—not near long enough."

"They shot Marty, didn't they," she finally said.

"Yes. We lost a good boy." He was heartsick thinking of the youth's demise.

"Like a son, if I ever have a son, I want him to grow up and be like Marty, Slocum." She sat up and used her fingers to comb her hair back from her face.

"I understand. Evelyn, we need to ride back to camp. Can you make it?"

"Yes."

"I'll help you in the saddle."

"I'm too filthy to touch," she said as if realizing her squalid condition. "My clothes look like—dirty as a pig."

"There's a good stream down there," he said.

"Can we take time? I want to wash this filthy dress

and myself.'' She looked down at her stained dress and shook her head in dismay.

"Come on," he said, picking up the expensive wool trade blanket to take with them. He'd found it among Murdock's things for her to nap on.

She half-ran to the water's edge ahead of him. In her haste, she gathered her dress up and cleared it over her head. Then her shift and camisole came off and were tossed in a pile. In a flash of bare skin, she charged into the water on the run. A few yards into the stream, she turned and looked back at him. The clear water swirled around her snow-white thighs, and her pointed pink nipples shone in the afternoon sun.

"Join me?"

"I'm a-coming," he said, toeing off his boots as he admired her.

The cattle had spread out grazing, but bunching them proved easier than Slocum had dreamed. With the morning light peeking over the hills to the east, they were going over last-minutes orders for his shortened crew. She sat on the wagon seat, reins in hand, and listened to them.

"Clem rides swing with me?" Zeke said, going over his instructions as they considered the day ahead. "And you think you and Doug can handle drag and the sides?"

"Have to." Slocum shrugged. "She's driving the wagon, and Red's sleeping in it, and we're hitching the spare saddle horses to it."

"Red sure wasn't going to be much help today anyway," Clem said with a head shake.

"No, but at least Slocum's whiskey has him out of his misery," Zeke said.

"Zeke and Clem, head out and shape them up," Slocum said. "We ain't whipped yet and we're going to deliver these steers."

"By damn, I believe we are," Zeke said, and mounted up.

"You drive easy, Evelyn," Slocum said to her as she

released the brake. "You don't need to be miles ahead of us."

"I heard you," she said, and then wrinkled her upper lip to show him. She swung the high-steppers around in a jingle of harness, and the iron wheels sang as she headed down the wide swale. He hoped that she could handle the big horses as he watched the string of remounts trail behind.

He shook his head in dismay. There was so much for him to hope for every day on this drive. The cinch tight, he slapped down the left stirrup and swung aboard. Doug was already gathering up the slow cattle when he trotted out to join him. He sung the tail of his reata and rode around the perimeter to get them moving.

"Fort Robinson will be your new home!" he shouted at the casual steers getting up to stretch and then acting unmoved by his rope work.

The sun stood noon high when he saw Zeke coming at a high lope. What had happened? He charged out of the dust to meet him.

"What's wrong?" he asked, jerking down his bandanna.

"We've found the road to Fort Robinson. Sign says forty miles." Zeke pointed back to the south.

"Good news. Keep driving them. We're going to make it yet. That sounds like three days work or less."

After the drover left for his place up front, Slocum pushed his horse around to tell Doug the news.

"Whew, three days. I'm getting me a bath, a haircut, a shave, and say, have you ever been there?" The youth narrowed his eyes in serious questioning.

"Nope, never been there."

"I wondered if they have a whore house there, do you know?"

"I'll bet they do." He smiled at the youth.

"I may not need a full shave," Doug said, feeling the sides of his smooth face with his palm.

"We better get to work," Slocum said, and they

pulled up their dirt-coated masks and went to driving the slow steers. They were getting close. The notion comforted him as he rode back and forth in the thick cloud of dust and pushed the stragglers along.

JAKE LOGAN

TODAY'S HOTTEST ACTION WESTERN!